When Princess Dominique and Ethan return to Monteaux for the Christmas season, Dominique receives an unexpected holiday gift. A beautiful baby boy is left for her under the Christmas tree, along with a note requesting that she keep the baby safe.

Their search for the mother exposes a crack that tests their relationship and leads to international entanglements with dangerous consequences.

This book is a work of fiction. Names, characters, places, and incidents either are products of the author's imagination or are used fictitiously. Any resemblance to actual events or locales or persons, living or dead, is entirely coincidental.

Royal Conflict
Copyright © 2021 Josephine Valent
ISBN: 978-1-4874-3297-3
Cover art by Martine Jardin

Published by eXtasy Books Inc

Look for us online at:
www.eXtasybooks.com

ROYAL CONFLICT
ROYALS 2

BY

JOSEPHINE VALENT

DEDICATION

To all the readers of Royal Mission.

CHAPTER ONE

Princess Dominique looked up as Frederique Crane, head of palace security, appeared in the doorway to the parlor. "Please excuse the interruption, Your Majesty," he announced, holding a box covered with Christmas wrapping paper and decorated with ribbons and holly. With the gift in his arms, he fits in seamlessly with the two enormous wood carved holiday soldiers flanking the entrance, she mused. With the crackling fire, garlands and lights hung around the room, and peppermint martini, it couldn't have felt more like Christmas, and with Ethan there, it was sure to be a memorable first for them. She lowered her hand to his leg and felt a tiny spark of heat in her belly, a reminder of the intensity of his pull.

"Yes, Frederique?" King Victor answered. He set his glass of whiskey on the table beside him.

"Someone placed this gift under the Christmas tree in the entrance hall. It is addressed to Her Royal Highness, Dominique . . . and . . . well . . . I'm not sure what to do with it," he explained as he peered into the box.

"Who is it from?" Dominique asked.

"It does not state," he answered.

She glanced at the blank expressions of her father, Victor, and his wife, Lidia. "Andre? Francine?" she asked, turning to her brother and sister-in-law.

"Not us," Andre answered.

"Ethan," she said, lifting her hand to his arm. The definition of his muscle under her fingers didn't surprise her, nor

1

did the rise of heat it triggered. She pushed the impending urges aside. She would act on those later in the privacy of her wing, but just the thought had the cravings moving back to the surface. "Did you—"

He shook his head. "It's not from me."

She pushed herself up from the settee. "It's a little early for opening gifts. Christmas isn't for another few weeks, but seeing how there is no lid on the box, let's have a look. Come in, Frederique, bring it to me." She took a few steps as he strode toward her. She had to admit, as much as she preferred to wait for it to get closer to Christmas before opening gifts, her curiosity was getting the best of her.

When he reached her, he tilted the box, and she peered inside.

"Oh, my. Frederique." She stared down at the shock of dark curls, the chubby cheeks, and the button of a nose buried amid a cloud of pale blue blankets. She waited for a sign that the baby was alive, and when she saw a soft twitch in its lip, she released a relieved breath.

"I'm sorry," he responded quickly. "My instincts were to call Inspector Laroche immediately, but since the envelope had your name written on it, I thought . . . forgive me, I did not think."

She turned toward Ethan, and he sprang to his feet. He hurried to her side and lifted a hand to the box. "What the—" was all he managed when he looked inside. She didn't miss the smile that erupted across his face.

"What is it?" Victor demanded.

"It's a baby," she answered. She turned to Lidia and Francine. "Come see."

"Frederique, how can you not know who left it?" Ethan asked.

"We know it was not a stranger that simply walked in and put it under the tree. The palace is impenetrable. He had to have been placed there by someone authorized to enter the palace, such as an employee or a service provider. With the holiday decorating going on, there have been a lot of outsiders coming through. It is possible that someone from the decorating company left it. We are reviewing the video of the entrance hall to identify the person."

"An employee is more likely to know that Dominique arrived today," Ethan suggested.

"It must be a boy. He is swathed in blue. He is so precious," Lidia gushed as she gazed down into the box. "Francine, how old do you think he is?"

"Well, judging from his face and the size of the box, I'd say he's no more than four or five months."

"Frederique, did he come with any spare parts," Andre asked as he hovered over Francine, "such as diapers or formula."

"Andre, that's a horrible way to ask that question," Francine scolded. "He is not an object, but," she continued as she turned to Dominique, "you should have a bottle ready when this lovely little angel awakens. And I wouldn't lift him out of that box until you have that bottle."

"That didn't occur to me," she answered. "Frederique, can you call down to the kitchen and have them prepare a bottle right away?"

"Yes, Your Royal Highness, and should I call Inspector Laroche?" he asked as he handed the box to Ethan.

"Yes," Victor answered, joining them.

"No," Dominique snapped back. "Absolutely not."

"I agree with Dominique," Ethan said, peering into the box. "He could be a keeper."

"I'll let you discuss how to proceed while I order a bottle and check on how my staff is coming on identifying who left the baby," Frederique said as he retreated. "Oh," he said, handing an envelope to Dominique, "here is the envelope that was taped to the box."

"Surely you're not thinking of keeping him," Victor said, staring into the box. "Although I must admit, he is a fine-looking baby."

"Let me take a look at that," Andre said, taking the envelope from her.

"No, of course not, but I will not allow him to be passed around and placed somewhere for orphans. He is obviously loved and well cared for. Look at those cheeks," she said, looking into the box. "They are full, and there is not a mark on them. Look at those curls. They are combed and styled."

"But it's Christmas time. We and the staff are swamped around here."

"That is all the more reason we should look after this baby. The holidays are a time of giving. We should give him a safe place to be and good care."

"She is right, Victor," Lidia said.

"Well, I can't argue with that, but we should at least tell Inspector Laroche about this so he can find the mother."

"No. The police will treat her like a criminal for abandoning her baby. I think we should find her and speak to her first. We should give her a chance to explain and to help her if she needs help."

"Um . . . I think I agree with Dominique, Father," Andre said, holding up the unfolded paper from the envelope. "Whoever left this baby has asked that he be protected. Not taken care of. Not looked after. *Protected.* That word suggests risk, trouble. His mother may need protection, as well."

"What?" Dominique snatched the paper from Andre and read it aloud. *"Please protect my baby."*

"You know what happened last time when we used Inspector Laroche. He let the necklaces slip right through his fingers," Andre reminded them.

Dominique looked at Victor. "The baby will be safe here,

and we will find his mother." She turned to Ethan and met his gaze. There was agreement in his eyes. He would help her, but there was something else in his eyes she couldn't quite read.

"We can start with the video of the entrance hall," Ethan suggested as he looked at Victor.

"All right, all right," Victor responded with a nod. "We'll double security until this is figured out."

"He's starting to squirm," Ethan reported, glancing into the box.

"He's opening his eyes," Lidia remarked. "And look. He's stretching."

"And not a peep," Francine added. "He's not cranky when he wakes up."

"Oh, no. I think you spoke too soon," Dominique said when he began to whimper. "Is that bottle here yet?"

"You may want to check his diaper," Francine suggested. "We don't want him to get a rash, and if he needs changing, he'll be happier when you feed him."

"I'm going to need your help with that, Francine," she answered.

"You'll catch on," she replied, lifting him from the box. "Let me check him. I'll change him quickly so you can feed him before he starts crying."

"I'm going to finish my drink," Victor remarked and headed back to his chair.

"I'll join you, Father," Andre said. "I think the ladies have this handled."

"Frederique," Ethan called as he headed back to the settee. "Has your staff been able to identify the person who left the baby?"

"No, sir, they have not. The individual was wearing a hood obscuring their face. Whoever it was is obviously aware of the camera and its placement. We are questioning the staff now, to see if anyone can recognize the person from their build."

Dominique felt the heaviness press against her heart. If the mother was in danger, they were going to need to find her before whoever was after them did. She knew what it was like to lose a mother as a child, and she couldn't bear the thought of this little bundle of beauty growing up without his mother. Whatever trouble the mother had gotten them into, she was going to find her and help them get out of it. She glanced down at the baby over Francine's shoulder. "I promise you everything will be all right," she whispered.

"I've been waiting too long to be alone with you," Ethan said as he and Dominique entered her bedroom. He tucked an arm around her waist and pulled her into him, reigniting the tiny sparks of heat in her belly. "Next time we fly private, so I don't have to wait so long."

"Hmm, I heard that the longer one waits for something," she said, sliding her arms up his chest and feeling the heat simmering inside of him, "the more it is appreciated."

"Oh, I appreciate you, honey," he assured her and touched his lips to hers. She could taste his hunger. It fueled her own. "You don't have to worry about that."

"Good to know." She dragged her tongue across his lips and then pressed her lips to his. When she kissed him, she felt his erection, and the heat in her belly started to churn. She drew back and slid her arms down his chest. "You are an impatient man," she teased as she turned in his arms and pulled her shiny, dark hair to one side. "Do you think you could help me with my zipper?"

"I think I can handle that." As he glided the zipper down, the heat between them surged, and the hunger swelled. He slid his hands inside her dress and slipped it off her shoulders. When it fell to the floor, she closed her eyes. She felt his breath on her neck and tilted her head, and when he slid his hands down her arms and brushed his lips over her neck, she thought she would melt in his arms. Unable or unwilling to move, she wasn't sure which, she stood motionless while he continued to undress her. When he unhooked her bra and tossed it aside, a quick breath escaped from her lungs. He dragged his lips from her neck down her back, leaving a trail of soft kisses as he slid his hands down her body to her panties. When he pulled them down, the heat and the hunger raged inside her.

He lifted her in his arms and carried her to the bed. "Hurry," she whispered as he lowered her to it. He yanked his shirt over his head, tore his zipper loose, and let his pants and briefs drop to the floor. He kicked them aside and lowered himself on top of her.

When she spread her legs, he wasted no time entering her. A moan passed her lips before he covered them with his. He retreated and then filled her again. The heat flowed through them at a feverish pitch. She took what she needed and gave what she could.

When he whispered her name, his voice washed over her like a cool breeze on a sweltering night. "Yes," she answered, and when he plunged into her one last time, he took her into another universe, and a million lovely little, euphoric explosions hammered inside her.

CHAPTER TWO

By the time Ethan awoke, Dominique was awake and dressed. He watched her slide her feet into a pair of shoes as he pushed himself up and swung his legs over the side of the bed. Damn, he thought, feeling the stir in his gut. *What she can do to a man is a crime.* "Good morning," he said, keeping his gaze on her as she looked over.

A smile spread across her face, and she sauntered over to him. She leaned down and kissed him.

"Good morning," she replied as she straightened and looked down at him, ignoring the budding urge. "I thought you might like to sleep in. Would you like me to have some breakfast brought up?"

"No," he replied and dragged a hand through his hair. "I think I'll shower first. Where are you off to?"

"I'm going to check on the baby and then meet with Frederique. By the way," she continued, "I want to thank you for agreeing to help me figure out why the baby was left here. I realize this is supposed to be a vacation and that our plans are probably going to be disrupted to some extent. I appreciate your being all right with that."

"I don't mind," he replied with a grin and stood. "It's a nice preview." He wrapped an arm around her and drew her into him. "Besides, I know you'll make it up to me."

"I'll definitely make it up to you," she said and then cocked her head. "What do you mean by it's a nice preview?"

He shrugged. "You know, a look down the road." He dropped his arm when she took a step back, and he raised a

8

brow. "Problem?"

"I don't know." She turned and took a few strides from him and then turned and faced him again. "We haven't discussed having children, and I never really saw them in my future. Do you want children?"

"Yes, and lots of them."

"I didn't know that. I thought . . . I guess . . . I assumed that if you didn't have any children with your wife, you didn't want them."

"We never got to that point in our marriage. I assumed you wanted children because, well, who doesn't want children?"

"Me. I don't want children." The words struck him like a bullet to the chest. He saw the tears surface in her eyes as she stared at him. "Where does this leave us?"

"I don't know," he said with a shake of his head.

"What do we do?"

He was silent for a minute as he stared down at her. Her words were pretty damn definitive, and her eyes told him there was no room for negotiation. He knew himself well enough to know that if he gave up having children for her, he would end up resenting her. He also knew that would ultimately end the relationship, and there was no point in delaying the inevitable. That didn't leave them with much to work with, he figured.

"Regardless of where this leaves us and what we need to do about it, I think we should focus on what's going on with this baby if you still want my help." He sat down on the edge of the bed. "Once the shock of this settles, I suppose we can talk about it, if there's anything to talk about."

"All right. I guess." She nodded, taking a deep breath and fighting back the tears. "Shall we meet in the security office in about an hour?"

"I'll be there."

She turned, and he watched her walk out. When she closed

the door behind her, he pushed himself up, strolled over to the armoire, and removed a small box from a shelf. He opened the box and stared down at the diamond and platinum engagement ring that was to be her Christmas present.

He closed the lid on the box and held it in his hands as he thought about their conversation. She didn't say why she didn't want children, and he wondered what the reason was. It probably didn't matter. She seemed pretty resolute about it. "You jumped the gun on this one, Ethan," he muttered to himself and returned the ring to the shelf.

When he got to the security office, she was already watching the video of the entrance hall. He strolled in and leaned over her to better view the monitor. Her scent filled his lungs, and he felt the tug to his gut. He had decided after his shower that he was going to do his best to concentrate on the matter at hand and not dwell on the inevitable, so he forced himself to be pleasant.

"Good morning, Frederique," he said, sliding a chair beside hers. He sat down and watched a figure on the monitor place the box under the tree. It was clearly a female, he concluded. Slight build, feminine movement.

"Look," Dominique said, pointing at the figure. "She is wiping tears. She doesn't want to leave her baby. For some reason, she must feel that she has no choice."

"Have you been able to identify this person?" he asked, glancing over at Frederique as he sat at the controls.

"Good morning to you, sir, and indeed, we have," he responded. He clicked his mouse and nodded to another monitor. "Look there." A pictured identification badge flashed onto the screen. "She is Isabelle Louden, an attendant. Her shift started an hour ago, and she has not shown up for work."

"I don't recognize her," Dominique said.

"You wouldn't. She has been employed here for barely over four months. She was referred by another attendant,

Sarah Stowe. We've spoken to Ms. Stowe, and she knows very little about Ms. Louden. She referred Ms. Louden at the request of her sister, Charlotte Stowe, who is a student at the university in Klovia."

"Klovia. So Isabelle is from Klovia?" she asked.

"Possibly. According to our records, her prior address was an apartment near the university. We found an address for an Elaine Louden in the south of Klovia. Based on her age, she could be her mother."

"Do you have a current address for Isabelle?"

"Yes," he replied. "We have a local address that she provided as current at the time she applied for the position."

Ethan looked over as she turned to him. "Perhaps we should start looking for Isabelle there," she suggested.

"I have a few other interesting images for you to see," Frederique advised, nodding to a monitor. An image of a man appeared at the palace staff entrance. "One of my men guarding the staff entrance recalled this gentleman identifying himself as Ms. Louden's brother. He said he could not reach Ms. Louden on her phone and had to deliver some urgent news to her. The guard found the gentleman to be shifty, so he told him she was not there and turned him away. He then sent word to Ms. Louden in case the gentleman was legitimate, assuming she would know how to contact him if he was her brother."

Ethan studied the man. Dark-haired, dark-skinned, possibly of Arab descent, he concluded. He was quite a contrast to Isabelle Louden, who was blonde and fair-skinned. Possible sex trafficking, he thought. He would run the image through his system, he decided, and he started a mental list.

"This was captured fifteen minutes later," Frederique continued, as he flashed another image of what appeared to be a man of slight build leaving the front entrance of the palace wearing a large overcoat that swallowed him and a beret pulled down over his face. "And this was captured forty-five minutes after that," he added, as another image of the figure wearing the overcoat with a hood instead of the beret appeared entering the staff entrance.

"Is that—"

"It is," Frederique answered, cutting Dominique off in his excitement. "The guard confirmed it, and the computer shows that Ms. Louden's badge was used to exit from the front entrance and to re-enter through the staff entrance at the same time these images were captured. She probably left through the front entrance suspecting that whoever was asking about her was watching the staff entrance. And, look closely," he said, positioning the cursor on the front of the coat in the second image, "you can see the light blue color under the coat. That is the same blue color as the blanket in the box with the baby, and the hood is the same color as the one worn by the person who left the baby under the tree. There is no doubt that Ms. Louden left the baby."

"She is in trouble," Dominique muttered, yet the alarm in her voice was unmistakable.

"It appears so," Frederique agreed. "Under the circumstances, I think we should contact Inspector Laroche. This situation is not palace business and is beyond the scope of our responsibilities."

"No." Dominique's voice left no room for debate, and Ethan knew she was not going to let the baby leave the palace until she found his mother, he was reunited with her, and they were both safe. He didn't like the idea of her being involved with something as potentially dangerous as sex trafficking, if that was what Isabelle was mixed up in, but he would keep her safe.

"Frederique, can you email the images to me, along with Ms. Louden's most current address and that of the woman who may be her mother, as well as any address you have for

Charlotte Stowe?" he asked. He would run the images and information through his system. Hopefully, he'd get a few more clues on what was going on with Isabelle and her baby.

"Of course."

"I'm going to check out Isabelle's current address," Dominique announced as she slid her chair away from the monitor.

"Slow down," he said, grabbing the arm of the chair. "You can't go off half-cocked. You have to know what you're walking into."

"Ethan, the situation is dire. We probably don't have time to waste."

"All the more reason we must be prepared." He held onto the chair and looked over to Frederique. "Can you have someone study the videos from your outside cameras to see if there is any indication that the palace is under surveillance? Look for any vehicles parked for extended periods and any figures loitering around."

"Will do, sir."

He turned to Dominique and swung her chair around to face him. "Promise me that you won't go anywhere without me. I can't worry about you if I have to concentrate on what's going on with Isabelle and her baby."

"I promise, but—"

"No buts." His voice was firm. "No exceptions. It's my way all the way or no way at all."

"All right. No buts, no exceptions," she agreed. "Your way all the way."

He released his grip on her chair and pushed himself up. It is going to be tough to leave her, he thought. Real tough. "Frederique, one last thing."

"Yes, sir?"

"Can I count on you for backup? I know His Majesty has doubled security around here. Do you have any men to spare?"

"We are spread thin, but the safety of you and Princess Dominique are my responsibility. I will give you my best men. Let me know if they will need anything additional."

"Very good. I will."

He placed a loose arm around Dominique and ushered her from the office. "I need to call Lance. I wasn't planning on working, so I didn't bring any equipment with me to access the system." He hated to make the kid work overtime during the holiday season, but he knew Lance was always eager to do anything he asked. Besides, he knew he'd make it up to the kid.

"You can use my office in my wing or the study down here," she offered.

"I'll get started down here. It's closer, and the sooner we can start figuring this out, the better."

He followed her to the study, sorting out the priority of the items on his mental list along the way. He punched in the key for Lance's direct line when he reached the doorway and headed for the desk.

"Hey, boss. How's it going?" He answered on the first ring as he usually did.

"A situation has come up. I need you to get me some information."

"Is Dominique all right?" He was quick to ask, and Ethan heard the concern in his voice. He knew how fond he was of Dominique. He practically idolized her.

"Yes. She's fine. A young mother left her baby with her, and it appears the mother may be in some kind of trouble. I need you to help us figure this out."

"Awesome . . . I mean . . . that's too bad. Should I catch a plane out there to you? You know I'm good in the field, boss."

He couldn't hold back the grin that crossed his lips. The kid had gotten a taste of danger and remembered only the excitement of it. It appeared that he had long forgotten how he had almost shit his pants when he'd been under gunfire.

"Lance, your job does not involve field work. ESM Defense Tech, Inc. does not do undercover work, spy missions, or anything like that. Dominique's kidnapping was an exception. Stop getting your hopes up. I don't like to keep disappointing you. All I need from you is some information."

"Okay, boss, but if things get messy, I'm available."

"All right. Here's what I need." He gave him his assignments to run the images of Isabelle and the man claiming to be her brother through the system and gather whatever information he could pull up from the system on them and Charlotte Stowe. The information on the address Isabelle had given in her application as her current address was easy and quick to access, and he provided that immediately.

"Where can we start?" Dominique asked from across the desk when he finished his call.

"The current address provided by Isabelle. It's a small house owned by an elderly woman. Louise Bardot. Since she purchased the house forty years ago, the woman has been living there. There's no public record of Isabelle residing there."

"So it could be a false address she provided?"

"It could be, or she could live there with the woman. We'll start there. Then we'll contact Charlotte Stowe and see what she knows about Isabelle."

"Okay. I'll call for a car."

"We're going to need an inconspicuous car," he said, pushing back from the desk. "No *Rolls-Royce* and no driver. And I'm going to need to talk to Frederique first. There are a few things I'm going to need from him."

It didn't take long to get what they needed and be on their way. Ethan scoured the parked vehicles on the street as he crept up to the house and determined that none of them looked occupied. Nothing appeared unusual about the place, either. He cut the engine and glanced back to see their backup pull into a space not far behind them.

"Let's see if Mrs. Bardot can tell us anything," he said and opened his door. He circled the car and helped Dominique out, and then they headed up to the house.

"I hope she's home," she said as they stepped up to the door.

"That would be nice," he said and knocked on the door.

No one answered. "Mrs. Bardot?" he called out and knocked again. He scanned the street as Dominique stepped off the porch to peer into a window.

"She's here. She's lying on the floor." Panic laced her voice as she rushed back to the porch and tried the door. The handle clicked, and she flung the door open.

He pulled her back and shoved her behind him before she could clear the threshold, already regretting allowing her to come with him. His gun drawn, he whispered into his mic to their backup. As he pointed the barrel around the perimeter of the room, he shielded her, and they crept over to Mrs. Bardot. Her wrists and ankles were bound, and tape was across her mouth. Dominique knelt down next to her while he stood guard over them. One of their backup men came through the front door, his gun drawn. Ethan motioned to him to stay with Dominique and Mrs. Bardot.

He nodded in return, and when he stepped beside Dominique, Ethan crept out of the room.

He was in a bedroom when he heard Mrs. Bardot's cries and Dominique's attempts to calm her. He was glad she was alive. He looked around and surveyed the room. The bedroom had been ransacked. A bassinet was lying on its side, a pile of diapers was scattered over the floor, and the closet door was open with one of the hinges pulled out of the frame. Whoever was looking for Isabelle was not happy she was not there, he figured, and he hoped he could find her before they did.

Chapter Three

When Ethan returned to the living room, Mrs. Bardot was sitting in a chair wiping tears from her cheeks with trembling hands. The tape had been removed from her mouth and the bindings from her wrists and ankles. Dominique was sitting next to her with an arm around her. One of the security teams stood near them while the other was standing guard at the door. Both had their security badges displayed at their waists. They could easily pass for official police badges with a glance.

"You're safe now, Mrs. Bardot. Are you sure you are all right?" Dominique asked.

"Yes." She nodded. "I'm all right."

"Would you like us to take you to the hospital so a doctor can check you?" she offered.

"No, no," she answered, shaking her head. "Isabelle is in trouble. My tenant and her baby. The men who came here were looking for her. You must find her." The urgency in her voice was unmistakable, as was the fear in her eyes. He watched as the fear turned to confusion, then to recognition. "You look like Princess Dominique."

"Mrs. Bardot," he interrupted before Dominique could answer. The sooner he got her out of there, the better. It had been a mistake to allow her to come with him. If whoever was looking for Isabelle got wind that Dominique was looking for her, too, she could be in more danger. "My name is Ethan Moore. I am with the special forces division." *Formerly, but close enough to the truth.* "These are members of my security team."

At the moment, anyway. He hoped the badges along with the introduction would be enough that she would assume they were all with the police. "Can you tell me what happened to you?"

"Yes, officer." She nodded and squeezed Dominique's hand. "Thank you, miss." Then she looked up at him. "Two men came to my house last night. It was about eight o'clock. They asked to see Isabelle. Isabelle rents a room from me. She has a baby. They both live here with me. I told them she wasn't here, but they didn't believe me." She hesitated, and a tear spilled down her cheek.

"Mrs. Bardot, may I get you a glass of water?" Dominique asked.

"Yes, please. The kitchen is right through there," she replied with a nod toward a door as she wiped the tear away.

"I'll be right back."

When Dominique slid her arm from Mrs. Bardot's shoulders, he motioned to one of the guards to go with her. When she stood and disappeared from the room, Mrs. Bardot clasped her hands in her lap and stared down at them. It was obvious what had happened when she had told the men Isabelle wasn't there, and the toll on her was equally obvious. He decided he didn't need to make her relive it. He sat down on the sofa across from her and continued. "Mrs. Bardot, how long have you known Isabelle?"

"About five months. She had just had little Liam when she answered my ad for a room for rent. I felt so sorry for her. She was all alone. She had nobody, and she was starting a new job. She needed someone to watch Liam while she worked. I thought I could help her get on her feet. An infant sleeps mostly, and I thought I could watch Liam until he got to be too much for me."

"Here you go," Dominique said, handing her the glass of water and sitting back down next to her.

"Thank you," she said and took a drink.

"Do you know where Isabelle is, Mrs. Bardot?" he asked and watched as the fear resurfaced.

"No," she shook her head. "Isabelle came home in the middle of the day yesterday, which is unusual. She was in a hurry and very upset about something. She said she had to take Liam somewhere. She didn't say where. I asked her if something was wrong or if something had happened. She didn't answer me. She just kept telling me to go visit my sister. She was very insistent that I spend a few days with my sister. Then she threw some of Liam's things in a bag and left." She glanced at Dominique, then back at him. "I hope they are all right. I hope those men haven't found them."

"Do you know who Isabelle might call if she needed help?" he asked.

"No. She has nobody that I am aware of."

"Do you know who Liam's father is?"

"No. Isabelle told me that his father died before he was born."

He took the photo of the man that had appeared at the staff entrance asking about Isabelle from his pocket and showed it to her. "Do you recognize this man?"

"That's one of the men that came here last night and tied me up. He's the one that asked about Isabelle."

"Did he say or give you any indication of why he was looking for her?"

"No. They pushed their way in when I opened the door and asked where Isabelle was. I told them she wasn't here, and then they tied me up and went through the house. When they were done, they left without saying anything else."

He glanced at the guard by the door and raised a brow. The man shook his head in response. There was no one watching the house. "Mrs. Bardot, it is possible that the men could come back if they can't find Isabelle. It might be safer if you stay with your sister for a few days. Can you tell me where she lives?"

"Yes. She lives here in Monteaux. On the west side."

"We can take you there, so we are sure that you are not followed. Would you like us to do that?"

"Oh, yes," she replied as she tried to push herself up. "I have to pack a few things if you wouldn't mind waiting."

"I'll help you," Dominique offered and helped her to her feet. Within ten minutes, the guards were ushering her to their car.

"We are no closer to finding Isabelle," Dominique said while he made sure she was safely inside the car. He scanned the street when the guards pulled from the curb and then strolled to the driver's side. There was no sign of anyone sitting in a parked vehicle and no sign that the guards' car was being followed. He lowered himself inside the car and turned the ignition. "We have no clue as to where Isabelle could have gone," she continued.

"Be patient," he said, glancing over. "At least we know that as of eight o'clock last night, whoever is after Isabelle hadn't found her." He looked down when his phone rang. "And we may know more now. Lance, what have you got?" he asked as he answered.

"Boss, the girl, Isabelle Louden. There's not much on her. Her prior address is an apartment just off campus from the university in Klovia. She dropped out before finishing, but the weird thing is that she had great grades and was only two classes away from graduating when she dropped out. The only other address I found for her is her mother's address. I haven't been able to find any documents on the baby. No hospital birth record, no government birth record. Nothing."

"Did you find any relatives other than her mother?"

"Her father died when she was ten. She was an only child. She had an uncle on her father's side, but he died two years ago. No one on her mother's side. The other girl, Charlotte Stowe, lived across the hall in the same apartment building as Isabelle. She's still attending the university and still lives in the same apartment."

"What about the guy claiming to be her brother?"

"No relation to her. His name is Bashir Fasil. He's on the staff of the Quam embassy located in Klovia. He lives in a swanky hotel in Klovia owned by Masoud Aziz, an ambassador from Quam who works at the embassy. Masoud has a son named Hashim, who also lives at the hotel. There's a total of four staff members from the Quam embassy that live at the hotel with Masoud and his son. He and his son occupy the entire top floor. The four staff members occupy part of the next floor down."

"Anything else?"

"Masoud and Hashim Aziz own palaces in Quam. They both travel back and forth a few times a year."

"Does anyone from the embassy in Klovia have any connection with Isabelle?"

"Not that I've been able to determine at this point."

"Email me the details of what you have. I'll let you know what else I want."

"Right, boss."

"It sounds like Charlotte Stowe is still next on our list," Dominique said. "The university in Klovia is about five hours over the border. We can fly and be there in under an hour."

He glanced over at her. The silky hair and the red lips were definitely making things difficult for him, and it wasn't going to get any easier if she was with him for the rest of the day. He needed a break from her. Besides, after the scare at Mrs. Bardot's, he wasn't willing to take any more chances with her.

"It's not a good idea for you to come with me to Klovia," he told her. "People on this side of the world easily recognize you, and it's best that whoever is after Isabelle does not know that you are involved in trying to find her. It could put you in danger and increase their efforts to find her."

Her silence told him she was considering his suggestion.

"I'd like to stay in Klovia overnight after I speak with Charlotte Stowe and see if I can find out more about Bashir Fasil and what his connection is to Isabelle," he added, hoping it would tip the scale in convincing her to stay in Monteaux.

"All right," she agreed, but he could tell by her frown that she was not happy. "I don't want to be a distraction to you if you have to worry about someone recognizing me, and I don't want to put Isabelle in any more danger than she is already in, but I want you to keep in touch with me and let me know as soon as you learn anything that will help us find Isabelle or determine what kind of trouble she is in."

"Understood." He turned onto the drive to LaBuerge Palace and proceeded to a rear entrance.

"I'll have my father's secretary purchase a ticket for a flight to Klovia, assuming you don't want the royal plane landing there, and make reservations at a hotel. Will you be taking someone from security with you?" she asked once they were inside.

"No. I shouldn't need any backup. I'd like a reservation at the hotel where Fasil is living. I'll give you the name as soon as I check my email from Lance." He shoved his hands in his pockets to resist the urge to touch her. "I'm going upstairs to throw a few things in a bag."

She nodded, and he watched as she walked away, pleased to know he wouldn't have to worry about her being in Klovia, yet disappointed he was going to be away from her for the night. It was good practice, he figured, as the thought of being permanently away from her started to gnaw at his insides.

When he reached her suite, he checked his phone to see if Lance had emailed the information. The kid is fast, he thought as he searched the email for the hotel's name and then texted it to Dominique. He's thorough, too, he thought as he flipped through the photographs of Masoud, Hashim, Fasil, and the three other embassy staff members. Hashim looked. impeccably groomed dark slicked-back hair, gold chains hanging from his neck, shirt unbuttoned to his navel. He swiped to the following photograph. Charlotte Stowe. She was young and pretty.

"If you're going to be doing any spying on these men living at the hotel, please be careful," Dominique said as she entered her suite.

"Trust me," he replied, walking up to her. "I will be."

"I'll help you pack. You have thirty minutes before you have to leave."

"Damn," he said, pulling her close, unable to resist the urge. "I'm missing you already." He felt the warmth, but he felt the awkwardness, as well.

"I know," she said. "Me, too."

CHAPTER FOUR

From his small table in the middle of the bustling student union, Ethan watched a petite figure making her way toward him through the throng of college students. She appeared nervous, and other than the occasional glance over her shoulder, she walked with her head down and her face partially concealed by her loose, dark hair. As she got closer, he recognized her from the photograph. Charlotte Stowe. As she approached the table, he saw that her eyes were red and swollen. The bruise on her cheek that was beginning to heal didn't go unnoticed by him, and he suspected there were more behind the turtle neck and under the sleeves of her red sweater.

"Mr. Moore?" Her voice was soft and full of trepidation. She looked younger in person than she did in the photograph. She could easily be mistaken to be in junior high school, he thought.

"Ms. Stowe." He pushed himself up, pulled out a chair, and gestured for her to sit. "Thank you for agreeing to meet me."

"I don't know if I can help." She took a quick look behind her, then sat down.

"It's a bit loud in here," he said. "I'd be happy to take you somewhere quieter and less hectic. There's a nice restaurant —"

"No. Thank you." She shook her head. "I prefer to stay on campus."

"That's perfectly fine," he replied. He was going to have to assuage that anxiety and get her to relax. She wasn't going to open up if she wasn't comfortable with him and didn't trust him. "May I buy you lunch? The line looks like it's moving along at the pizza counter."

"Thank you. Yes."

"Pepperoni?" He stood and smiled down at her.

When she nodded, he saw a hint of a smile cross over her face.

"I'll be right back," he said and strolled over to the line. She knows something, he thought. She was clearly nervous and upset about something before she got there. He scanned the room for anything suspicious or out of the ordinary, but he saw nothing but swarms of students eating, reading, laughing, and doing the expected. He kept an eye on her as he made his way to the counter. He noticed she seemed to be relaxing a bit as she let herself rest against the back of the chair.

He purchased a whole pizza and a couple of sodas and then headed back to the table.

"I hope you're hungry," he said, setting the box on the table. He untwisted the cap on one of the bottles of soda, placed it before her, and then opened the box's lid and served her a slice. Take your time, he told himself. No need to rush her.

"What can you tell me about Isabelle?" he asked after she finished the second slice of pizza.

She pushed her paper plate aside and hesitated a moment before dropping her gaze from his. "It's my fault Isabelle is missing."

"How is it your fault?"

She tucked her arms over her chest and closed her fingers around her arms. "Hashim and Bashir were waiting for me outside of my apartment a couple of days ago. They made me get in a van, and then they drove me around. They kept asking me if Isabelle had the baby and where she was. I told them that she lost the baby and that I didn't know where she was."

"What is their connection to Isabelle?"

She lifted her head and looked up at him. "You don't know?"

"I know very little. I was hoping you could fill me in enough to help me find Isabelle so we can protect her."

"Hashim likes college girls. He hangs around the bars and clubs we go to. Last year, Isabelle and I were at a club, and Hashim came. He had his sights set on her." She dropped her head, shook it. "I warned her not to get involved with him, but she didn't listen. They started dating, and he monopolized her time. I'd see her when she would come back to her apartment to change or get her computer for class. I never saw them at the bars or clubs students frequent once they were dating. I guess he took her other places."

"Why did you warn her? What did you know about him?"

She shrugged. "I didn't know much about him. I just didn't like him. He was controlling and arrogant. He acted like he was better than everyone else." She lifted her head and met his gaze. "Like he was untouchable."

"He is the father of Isabelle's baby?"

She nodded. "When she got pregnant, she realized she should have listened to me. She found out he had been cheating on her almost the entire time they had been dating. She tried to keep the pregnancy from him and cut things off, but when he found out she was pregnant, he tried to convince her to move to Quam. She was almost eight months pregnant by then. She refused, and he became very insistent. He told her that he owned her and the baby, and they had to live in Quam. He warned her that he would kill her if she didn't obey him. He told her that he had already killed the mother of one of his children for going against his wishes."

"So she ran away?"

"Yes. I helped her. We both thought he wouldn't find her if she left the country. We thought she would be safe once she was out of Klovia."

27

"And you thought she would be safe in Monteaux."

"Yes. I drove her so there would be no trace of her travel. She lived very quietly there. She had some money left from her inheritance, so she stayed in a hotel under a false name until she had the baby. She avoided the hospital, found a midwife to deliver him, and did not register his birth. Then she rented a room in someone's house, so she didn't have to have a formal lease, and she got a job at the palace away from the public."

"Why did Hashim come to you now?"

"I made a mistake. Isabelle and I agreed when I left Monteaux that we would cut off all ties until I graduated from college and moved away from my apartment so she and the baby would stay safe. And we did." He watched as the tears filled her eyes. "I wanted to do more for her. She'd had such a terrible life. Her father died when she was young, and then her mother remarried. She didn't get along with her mother or stepfather and lived on the streets for a while before her uncle took her in. When she was old enough, she had access to an inheritance for college. It was her only break in life, and she was adamant that she wouldn't waste it. She's only two classes short of getting her degree. I registered for two classes in her name a couple of weeks ago. I was going to take the classes for her and surprise her with her diploma."

"Hashim found out she was registered?"

When she nodded, the tears flowed like a river in a storm. He slid her chair next to his and wrapped an arm around her, and then he took a handkerchief from his pocket and handed it to her. She buried her head in his chest, and he wrapped a second arm across her.

"He found out somehow," she managed between sobs. "He didn't believe that she didn't have the baby and that I didn't know where she was. He called me a liar and punched me in the face. I kept telling him I didn't know anything, and he kept beating me. I took as much as I could."

"You are not to blame for what's happened." The anger boiled inside him as he imagined how hard she had probably fought to keep Isabelle and her baby safe and how terrified she must have been.

"Yes, I am. I was afraid he was going to kill me, so I told him Isabelle was in Monteaux."

"He would have found her eventually, and Isabelle and Liam will never be safe as long as he is looking for them." The bastard was leaving a lot of suffering in his wake, and he was going to end it. And make him pay for it. "Is there anything you can tell me to help me find Isabelle before he does? Would your cousin know where she is?"

"No. She doesn't know anything except that Isabelle needed a job. I was afraid if she knew anything else, she wouldn't recommend Isabelle for a position at the palace." She lifted her head and dabbed at her tears.

He withdrew an arm but kept one around her as he looked down at her. "Take a deep breath."

She nodded and looked up at him. "I can tell you that Isabelle loves her baby more than anything else. She never considered abortion or adoption, and she is never going to let Hashim end up with him."

"Can you tell me anything more about Hashim and this girl he claims to have killed?"

"No. As far as I know, he never told Isabelle who she was. But about three years ago, the daughter of President Balan vanished. After what happened with Isabelle, I always wondered if Hashim had anything to do with her disappearance."

That was speculation on her part, but he would keep it in mind. He needed to look at the facts, and those were that Hashim Aziz had threatened to kill Isabelle, had confessed to killing another girl, and he and his buddy, Bashir Fasil, had terrorized Mrs. Bardot and Charlotte.

"All right." He gave Charlotte a squeeze, then drew his arm from around her. "Thank you for meeting with me. After what you've been through, it was brave of you to meet with me. I'm going to make sure you are not followed back to your apartment, and I'm going to put my phone number in your phone. I want you to call me if you hear from Hashim again or if you hear from any of his friends."

He entered his number in her phone, and when she left, he followed her to her apartment. No one else had followed her. Hashim had gotten the information he was looking for from her. She was probably safe from him for now, he figured, and he called Lance as he hailed a cab to head back to the hotel.

CHAPTER FIVE

"Hey, boss," Lance answered on the first ring. "I'm still working on the connection between Isabelle and someone at the embassy."

"Don't waste your time on that. I got my answer. I need you to see if there were any missing person reports filed in the last three years for any females attending the university in Klovia and if the cases were resolved. And see what you can find out about President Balan's daughter who disappeared."

"President Balan?"

"President of Klovia."

"Oh, yeah, right. I'm on it."

"One more thing. Find out where Hashim Aziz's palace is in Quam and see if there's any kind of security system with cameras there that you can access."

"Okay, what are you looking for in the palace? Anything specific?"

"Yeah, but it's a long shot, I think. See if there are any young women, twenty to twenty-five years old, living there, and any young children, toddler age."

"Got it, boss. I'll let you know."

"Good. Later." He tucked his phone in his pocket, handed the driver a few bills, and stepped onto the curb. He had a feeling Hashim and his sidekick Bashir Fasil might be in Monteaux looking for Isabelle. He needed to get back there, but first, he'd see what he could find out there about Hashim, if anything.

He headed into the hotel bar and took a quick look around.

It was midday and not that busy. Most of the customers were being tended to by waitresses. There were only two people at the bar, making it likely that he might be able to have a conversation with a bartender. He strolled up to the bar and took a seat.

A second bartender came out from the back carrying a tray of clean highball glasses. She set the tray down behind the bar when she spotted him and walked over.

He nodded. "How are you doing?" he asked.

"I'm supposed to ask you that question," she said with a smile. "What can I get you?"

"Whiskey. On the rocks."

"Any particular brand?"

"What have you got?" It didn't matter. He didn't plan on drinking more than a few sips. He wasn't there for the whiskey. He was there for information.

"*Bulleit . . . Kavalan . . . Yamazaki—*"

"That one will do."

"All right. I'll be right back with that." He watched as she strode to the shelves of liquor against the wall opposite the bar, selected a bottle, and then brought it to the bar. She didn't waste time with the glass and ice cubes and was back in under two minutes, he guessed.

"Are you going to answer my question?" he asked as she set the glass on the bar.

"What question?" she asked, looking confused.

"How are you doing," he said and lifted the glass to his lips.

"Oh." A smile erupted across her face. "Do you want the small-talk answer or the honest answer?"

"I prefer the honest answer," he replied and set his glass down.

She glanced down the bar, and he followed her line of sight. The second bartender was engaged with the only other two customers at the bar. She leaned against the bar and looked back at him. "I work here full time and had to work an extra shift last night because one of the other bartenders quit without notice. I'm exhausted and not happy."

"Aren't there laws against that?"

"There are no laws here. The owner thinks the laws don't apply to him. You work when they tell you to work and collect your pittance. If you complain, you get fired. When you're ready to quit, you quit on payday, or you risk not getting paid your final wages."

"Sounds like your boss is a real gem," he quipped.

"He's a tyrant," she said, the disgust in her voice evident.

"Why don't you get another job?"

"I need to pay my bills, and jobs are scarce right now." She shifted her weight and then leaned in a little closer. "I'm taking courses at the university. This job is only temporary until I get my degree. Then I can get a better job with a better employer."

He reached for a hundred euro banknote in his pocket and pulled it out. He slid it onto the bar and placed his glass on top of it. "Will this help you pay your bills?"

She pushed back from the bar with a frown. "Sir, I do not do that sort of thing."

He smiled. "This is not for that. It is for information only. And your promise to keep our conversation between us."

Her gaze dropped to the note, then lifted back to his as she leaned back down. "What kind of information?"

"Hashim Aziz," he said, keeping his gaze on hers, reading her. She wasn't fond of Masoud Aziz, and he was willing to bet she wasn't fond of his son.

"He has a suite on the top floor that he lives in. He doesn't come through the lobby or in here often. I understand he mostly uses a private entrance in the rear of the hotel to come and go. It supposedly leads to a private garage where he and his father keep their cars." She rolled her eyes as she continued. "He doesn't walk. He swaggers. He's so arrogant. It's offensive."

"What have you heard about his dating habits? The girls he's dated."

"Well, it's common knowledge that he goes after young college girls. That seems to be his taste. He charms the pants off them, literally, and when he gets bored with them, he moves on to the next one."

"Have you ever heard of anyone he's dated disappearing?"

"I haven't heard that, but I have heard rumors that he has wives. If he does, I don't think they live here. I've heard he takes the girls he's dating upstairs, and I don't think he'd do that if he had wives living up there." She shrugged. "But you never know."

"Have you ever heard about any of the girls he's dated getting pregnant?"

"I haven't heard that, but I wouldn't be surprised. Based on the number of girls I hear he's dated over the years, odds are at least one of them got pregnant. Listen, I think you might want to talk to someone on the cleaning staff. I hear they've got maids up there all day long cleaning up after him. I'm sure they've seen a lot, including the girls that have come and gone. And they're professional gossipers. They know everything that goes on in this hotel."

He lifted his glass, tossed her a wink, and took a sip. When she slid the euro note off the bar, he headed up to his room. Inside, he strode over to the window and looked out over the city.

He allowed his thoughts to drift to Dominique. What was supposed to be the best Christmas of his life was turning out to be the worst. He should have never given in with her. He'd been weak. No, he corrected himself. He'd been weak and stupid. He'd acted like a little pimple-faced kid hitting puberty and getting laid for the first time. He'd lost all self-control with her. All willpower. All discipline. And when he'd gotten a taste of her, there was no turning back. He shook his head as he pondered the pouty lips, silky flesh, perfect breasts, and long legs. And the raw, primal passion. His appetite for her was insatiable, and his love for her ran deep. It wasn't going to be easy to walk away from her.

He strolled over to the sofa and tried to shake her from his mind. He told himself that he had to get back to the purpose of his trip. He'd deal with the situation with Dominique when he got back to Monteux. He pulled out his phone and checked his email. He stared at the young faces of the three girls in the photographs that Lance had sent him. One was the daughter of President Balan. She was just sixteen when she had gone missing three years before. Her hair was blonde like Isabelle's. The other two girls didn't look much older than the President's daughter, though their hair was darker. One had gone missing sixteen months after the President's daughter, and the most recent girl had gone missing ten months after that. He felt a tug at his heart when he thought about what their parents must have gone through and probably still were going through. He was sure a day didn't go by that their parents didn't mourn for them.

He reached for the receiver to the hotel phone and hit the button for housekeeping. When someone answered, he requested that some clean towels be sent up. He invited the maid in when she delivered the towels. It seemed that no one there had any loyalty to Masoud or Hashim Aziz. Although the maid hadn't been employed there long enough to recognize any of the girls, she told him that her cousin had worked at the hotel for four years. She was sure she had information because she had been assigned to clean the suites on the top floor. Her shift started the following day, and she promised her cousin would come to his room and talk to him before her shift began.

Assuming Hashim didn't do much cooking, he next placed an order for an early dinner. When the server told him he had been working there for five years and Ethan saw him look at the hundred euro banknote he'd set on the table next to the tray, Ethan knew he was going to be more than willing to talk about the son of his boss.

"Have a seat," he said, pulling a chair from the table. When he sat down, he showed him the photograph of President Balan's daughter and sat down across from him. "Do you know who she is?"

"Of course, everybody knows who she is," he said. "That's Bianca Balan, the president's daughter. She went missing a few years ago."

"Have you ever seen her with Hashim or in his suite?"

"I heard rumors that she dated him, but I've never seen her with him or upstairs. It's no secret that her father was opposed to their dating. So, if they dated, he most likely kept a really low profile with her."

"Do you know why her father was opposed to them dating?"

He shrugged. "She was young. He's a player. I don't know."

He placed the photographs of the other two missing girls on the table. "Have you seen either of these girls with Hashim?"

He studied their pictures and nodded. "Yes, both of them. This one," he said, pointing at one of the photographs, "I saw about a year ago in Hashim's suite. This one," he said, pointing at the other photograph, "maybe a year before that. It's hard to say exactly. Hashim often juggles more than one girl at a time."

"How are you so sure about these girls then?"

"Well," he began with a grin, "I check out the girls I see up there, and I don't forget a face. And this girl," he continued, sliding one of the photographs closer, "I remember seeing her picture in the news. She was reported missing. And this one, the police questioned me about."

"What kind of questions did they ask?"

"Same ones you're asking. Had I seen her with Hashim or in his suite?"

"What did you tell them?"

"Nothing. The employees here are required to be discreet. I didn't want to get fired."

"Why were the police asking you about her?"

"I don't know. They didn't say. I assumed they were looking for her because she had stolen money or something from Hashim. He's rich. I'm sure he keeps a lot of money up there."

"What about the other girl that went missing? Did the police ever ask you about her?"

"No."

"How long after you had seen her in Hashim's suite did you see her picture in the news?"

"She had been a regular visitor in his suite for a few months. It was probably about a week after the last time I had seen her up there."

"How about her?" he asked, showing him a photograph of Isabelle.

"Yes, I've seen her. More recently. Probably the last time was about eight months ago."

"Do you know if any of these girls were pregnant?"

"I wouldn't know that." He picked up the photograph of the girl he'd seen in the news. "This one, though, did start to get a little chunky right before she went missing."

"Do you have any idea where any of these girls are?"

He shrugged. "No idea."

"Have you ever heard Hashim talking about any of these girls or what happened to them?"

"No, but I did hear him say something to one of his buddies about his girlfriends in Quam. I guess he's a player there, too."

"Okay, thanks." The server had connected the two missing girls to Hashim around the time of their disappearance. That was good. If they were pregnant when they went missing, there was a possibility that they could be in Quam, based on what Charlotte had told him about Isabelle.

"Is that it?" he asked, pushing back from the table. He picked up the banknote and stuffed it in his pocket. He stood, turned to leave, and then turned around. "Uh . . . listen . . . you know —"

"Discreet." Ethan stood, circled the table, and placed a reassuring hand on his shoulder as he accompanied him to the door. "This conversation stays between you and me."

He looked at his watch and decided to call Dominique as he had promised, and he couldn't deny that he was looking forward to hearing her voice. He strolled into the bedroom and sat on the edge of the bed as he entered her number.

"Hello," she answered after the first ring. "How is it going there? Are you safe?"

"I'm safe, and it's been somewhat productive," he replied and filled her in on his conversations. "How are things going there?"

"It's been uneventful," she replied, "which is good, considering that the two men looking for Isabelle are still watching the palace, which is also good, since that means they haven't found her yet."

"I think we're missing something about Isabelle, and I can't figure it out."

"What makes you think we're missing something?" she asked.

"I don't know. Maybe it will come to me in the morning after I get some sleep."

"I'll think about what we know. Maybe something will come to me."

"I think I'm going to get some dinner," he lied, "and call it an early night."

"All right. I'll see you tomorrow, then."

"Yeah, I'll see you tomorrow," he said and hung up. "Damn," he muttered and tossed his phone onto the bed. The tension between them was so thick he could have choked on it. He knew she felt it, too. And the awkwardness. Things were deteriorating between them fast.

Chapter Six

Ethan tossed his bag in the taxi and slid into the back seat. The maid had shown up as promised. As it turned out, Hashim and his guests were usually away when the maids cleaned his suite, except for one occasion when she had accidentally seen Bianca Balan sleeping in one of the bedrooms in Hashim's suite about a week before she disappeared. Yes, it has been a fruitful trip, he thought. He just hoped his suspicions panned out.

Dominique watched Liam while she waited for the nanny to return. Francine is right, she mused as she stared down at him. He is a happy baby. He made her wish she had been gifted with maternal instincts. But she hadn't been. In fact, it was quite the opposite. Having children and being responsible for them terrified her as much as the thought that she and Ethan had reached an impasse in their relationship pained her.

He had not minced words when he'd expressed his desire to have children. *Lots of them* was what he had said. And it hadn't gone unnoticed that their telephone conversation the evening before had been strained. It was clear that he was already distancing himself from her, and the thought of it sliced through her heart.

"Liam," she murmured as she reached down and caressed his chubby cheek. "Tell me, what cruel joke is the universe playing on me with you?" She smiled as he waved his arms, kicked his feet, and giggled up at her in response.

She listened when she heard footsteps as someone hurried through the entrance hall and looked up as they got closer. When Ethan strode through the parlor doors, her heart gave a little jolt. She was sure it was as much relief that he was safe as it was that she was happy to see him, as she knew their time together was limited.

"Welcome back," she said, feeling the awkwardness between them.

"It's good to be back," he replied. "I figured out what—well, hello, you little squirt," he said, his thought interrupted by Liam's babble. He lifted him from the baby bouncer. Holding him above his head, he laughed as Liam kicked and squealed. "You're in a good mood," he said and lowered him to his chest. He lifted him again.

"I'm waiting for the nanny to get back," she remarked, watching him with Liam. He was so comfortable, such a natural with him. The joy on his face was obvious as he played with Liam. She wished she could be as comfortable with children. "What were you about to say? What did you figure out?"

"We should probably meet with Frederique and discuss it. We're going to need his help to see if I'm right. Hey, little fellow," he said, lifting him up again and waiting for another squeal. When Liam delivered, he lowered him back down and handed him to her.

"Wait, I—"

"Relax. You've got him. I'm going upstairs to splash some water on my face and wash off some of this travel grime before we meet with Frederique," he said and then turned and strode from the room.

She fought the panic threatening to take over while she tried to balance a squirming Liam on her lap.

"You little wiggle worm," she managed and heard the fear

in her voice. She released a slow sigh and then inhaled a long breath. "My, you are fidgety." Trying to calm herself, she slid from the edge of the chair onto her knees and then set him on the carpet. She sat down next to him, releasing a relieved breath.

"What are you doing?" she asked as he rolled over. She felt an unexpected little hint of excitement as she recalled that rolling over was some sort of a milestone when her niece and nephew were babies. "Oh, my. You little monkey."

"I'm back," the nanny announced as she came through the doorway. "Did he get fussy?"

"No, I was just . . ." She stood and shook her head. "Never mind. He just rolled over. I think maybe you should know that."

"Oh, yes. I haven't seen him do that. I didn't know he could," the nanny responded as she plucked him from the floor. "We are going to have to be more careful and watch where we put him down."

"Yes," she said as she turned to leave. That makes sense, she thought, and she wondered if that would have occurred to her.

She decided to head up to her wing. She was too curious to hear what Ethan had figured out to wait to discuss it with Frederique. As she started up, little ripples of desire drifted through her, reminding her that she had missed him the evening before. She swallowed hard as she tried to stave them off. She certainly didn't need to be lusting after him when she needed to be preparing herself for his absence. Annoyed at her lack of control as the ripples persisted, she tried to ignore them. Unsuccessful and reaching her suite, she opened the door and stepped into the foyer. It was quiet, and as she closed the door, she wondered if she had missed him and if he was on his way to meet with Frederique.

She decided to check the bedroom to see if he was

unpacking his bag. Grabbing a piece of mail from the table, she headed through the foyer toward the hallway as she opened it.

When she heard a noise, she looked up. Surprised to see him standing in the hallway with just a towel draped around his shoulders, she stopped short. She couldn't help but stare as tiny droplets of water glistened across the cut of muscles. Any attempt to ignore the ripples was now even more useless.

He looked up and met her gaze. "I thought I'd take a quick shower," he said. "I didn't know you were coming up."

"I—I—" she stammered, looking for words, and then gave up as she felt herself surrender to her impulses, any sensible thoughts having slipped away. She continued toward him until only a breath of air separated them.

She sensed the tension inside him, but it was laced with passion. She felt any ability he may have had to resist her vanish. Whether he lost it or relinquished it, she didn't know.

She dragged the towel from his shoulders and let it fall to the floor. She saw his erection grow as she unzipped her skirt and pushed it and her panties down.

He lifted her up and guided her onto his penis when she stepped out of them. She felt his hands cup her buttocks as he held her at his waist. She closed her legs around him, and he shoved her against the wall. Holding her against it, he withdrew and then thrust himself inside her. She tightened her legs around him as he withdrew again and then braced herself against the wall, ready for the next assault. He plunged inside her, and the ripples turned to long, slow waves.

He spun around and carried her into her office. He lowered her to the edge of the desk and leaned over her as she lay back. He pulled back and then drove in again. With each drive, the waves intensified as he pushed her closer to the edge.

He slid her off the desk in one swift move, and she pushed him onto the settee. Straddling him, she took him in deep as she glided down the length of him. She pulled up, then lowered herself again, taking him all. The waves inside her escalated, and she took him deeper. When the waves crashed, she swore her heart stopped as she took him over the edge with her.

Breathless, she collapsed against him. When she heard him release a long, satisfying breath, she pushed herself off of him.

"Um . . . shall I let Frederique know we'll be down in, say, twenty minutes?" she asked, still at a loss for words.

He nodded, and as she turned and walked away, she felt his gaze on her. She couldn't help the slight smile that crossed her lips.

When they walked into the security office, Frederique was sitting in front of a couple of monitors watching video footage of various exits from the palace. "Have you found anything yet?" Ethan asked as he pulled a couple of chairs over for him and Dominique.

"What is he looking for?" she asked as she lowered herself to one of the chairs. She saw a flicker of excitement in Ethan's eyes as he took the other chair beside her and started to explain.

"From what Charlotte told me about Isabelle, it didn't make sense that she would abandon Liam, even with you where he was certain to be safe. And I couldn't help but think that she would want some kind of assurance that you wouldn't turn him over to the authorities."

"What are you saying?"

"I think Isabelle is hiding somewhere inside the palace. I asked Frederique to see if her badge showed that she had exited the palace after she had entered with Liam." He looked over at Frederique. "Frederique?"

"Her badge was not used to exit after she came back with Liam. I'm checking the exits now to see if she left without using her badge."

"I'm so glad you figured out that was what was bothering you," she said, turning to Ethan. "I'm going to look for her," she said, pushing up from the chair.

"We haven't confirmed it yet."

"I'll confirm it. I'll find her," she tossed over her shoulder as she grabbed a flashlight off a shelf and hurried out of the office. She pulled out her phone and entered Andre's number. He answered on the second ring.

"What can I do for you, sister? Is Ethan back?" he asked.

"Yes, and I need your help. He thinks Isabelle is hiding somewhere in the palace. I need you to help me find her. I need you to help me check all of the hiding places we used when we were children."

"What makes him think she's hiding here?"

"It doesn't matter. Can you help me?" She was already heading to the rear staircase.

"Of course. I can finish what I'm working on later. Where do you want me to start?"

"I'm going to the rear staircase, now, to check the south cellars. Can you check the east ones? I doubt she'd be hiding in the wine cellars. There would be too much traffic down there. So we can eliminate looking in the north cellars, and I doubt she'd be in the storage cellars. There's too much stacked in them, so we can eliminate looking in the west cellars."

"Yes. I'll check the east cellars and call you when I'm done."

She started her descent down the cold stone steps. When she reached the rear staircase, memories of her adventures and explorations with Andre came floating back. They had been pirates, archeologists, astronauts, and whatever else their imaginations had conjured up. She remembered the staircase being slightly wider as she recalled her and Andre sliding down the steps atop a mattress and nearly cracking their skulls against the heavy wooden door at the bottom. It had been a fun ride, but Andre had paid the price for that escapade. As she made her way further down, she recalled the earthy aroma and distinct drop in temperature as she was hit with them. It seemed like a lifetime ago since she had been in the cellar.

Stepping from the last stair, she lowered the lever and pushed open the door. Only a trickle of light fell into the room. She felt along the wall and flipped a light switch. It was the only electricity down there, and the bulb dangling from the ceiling cast only a dim light in the room. She took a few steps and then looked around the room. It had been mostly empty when they had played there years ago. Now, there were some old bookcases, plastic containers, and other odds and ends neatly stacked against a wall. She switched on the flashlight and directed the beam down one of the long hallways that extended further beneath the palace. It was empty, and the doors along it were closed. Next, she shined the light down the other hallway. It, too, was empty, and the doors closed. She chose the hallway on the right and walked a few yards toward it. It was cold in the cellar, and she wished she had thought to bring a jacket.

When she entered the hallway, she contemplated how far through the labyrinth of passages she should search and wondered if Isabelle knew the cellars were the best places to hide. The doors were staggered, and the first one she reached was on her left. She wrapped her fingers around the knob and nudged the door open. She shined the light around the perimeter of the room. It was empty. She closed the door and proceeded to the next one down.

She closed her hand around the knob and pushed the door open. The beam from the flashlight caught something move, startling her.

"Isabelle?" she asked as she entered the chamber. She

focused on the object and moved toward it.

"Isabelle?" she asked again when there was no answer and then knelt down beside what she saw was a figure huddled in the corner under a blanket. She lifted the blanket exposing the frightened face of a young girl. When the girl looked up, she nodded.

She offered her a warm smile and placed an arm across her shoulders. "It's okay. We'll keep you safe, too," she said. "Come with me."

CHAPTER SEVEN

With Isabelle and Liam safely inside the palace, King Victor insisted that a meeting be arranged to discuss the predicament in which Dominique had placed the family and that Inspector Laroche be called in to participate. The entire family, Ethan, Isabelle, Frederique, and Inspector Laroche, gathered around the table in the study. Dominique dragged her gaze over their faces. The scowl on Laroche's face told her he wasn't happy about not being called in sooner.

"We can only arrest Hashim Aziz if he is in Monteaux and committed a crime here. We do not know if he is here, and it is questionable whether Hashim committed a crime here. We don't know if he was with Bashir Fasil when Fasil was asking for Isabelle, and we have no proof that such was an attempt to kidnap her and her baby," Inspector Laroche explained. "And if he was with Fasil when Fasil tied up Louise Bardot, and we arrest him for that," he shook his head," that is not going to keep Isabelle safe for long, if at all."

"Excuse me," Ethan said, answering his phone and then stepping out of the room.

"Father, can't you talk to President Balan and persuade him to do something? Hashim assaulted Charlotte Stowe in his country and threatened to kill Isabelle there. And Hashim was dating those college girls when they disappeared. Both the hotel server and the maid can verify that."

"Allow me, sir," Inspector Laroche said. "Anything Charlotte and Isabelle say will be controverted by Hashim and his cohorts. It will be a she said, he said situation. It would be risky for Charlotte and Isabelle to pursue charges under those circumstances. And," he continued, "as far as the college girls that went missing, anything the server or the maid says—if they are even willing to talk, which is doubtful—there is no proof that Hashim had anything to do with their disappearance. Dating them when they disappeared does not equate with murdering them."

"None of that matters, anyway," Victor said with a dismissive wave of his hand. "Masoud Aziz is a diplomat in Klovia. As his son, Hashim has diplomatic immunity there. Bringing this information to President Balan's attention would only cause an international incident which I do not want to be in the middle of."

Dominique felt the weight of frustration begin to push down on her as she began to question whether there was a solution for Isabelle and Liam.

"I just received some additional information," Ethan announced as he strode back into the room.

Dominique lifted her gaze to him, hoping he had information that Laroche and her father would find significant enough to be able to use to help Isabelle.

"Let's hear it," Andre said, "because what Inspector Laroche and my father just explained is rather disappointing."

"I think the information I have might be a little more encouraging and may be conducive to finding a solution for Isabelle," he said as he returned to his chair and continued. "We were able to access the security cameras at Hashim Aziz's palace in Quam. It looks like other than staff, there are two young women and three babies or toddlers living there. We ran photos made from the videos through our facial recognition program, but the video quality is not good, so the photos are not good. Our system reported a possible match to Bianca Balan, and the other one to Dorina Eder, one of the college girls reported as missing. But the match was not one hundred per-cent. So we cannot say with certainty that Bianca Balan and Dorina Eder are the girls there."

"I'd say that's a bit more encouraging," Andre agreed.

"Now, what do you say, Father?" Dominique asked, her hopes rising.

"Slow down," Ethan warned. "We haven't been able to confirm that either of these women is who we think they are or whether they are there against their will. "Even if they are Bianca Balan and Dorina Eder, they may have gone to Quam voluntarily and are living there willingly."

"Assuming they are Bianca and Dorina, they were reported as missing," Dominique reminded him. "If they were there voluntarily, don't you think they would be in touch with their families?"

"Not necessarily," Inspector Laroche replied. "Mr. Moore said earlier that President Balan was opposed to his daugh-ter's involvement with Hashim and that she kept it a secret. She may still be keeping it a secret, and we know nothing about the other young woman. We need to work with facts."

"And for all we know, they could be in touch with their families," Andre added. "They may no longer be considered missing, and it was just never reported to the public."

"Father? What do you think?"

"Dominique, we are not certain that the women are Ms. Balan and the other missing girl. I am not going to do any-thing based on speculation, and I won't consider doing any-thing until their identities are confirmed and we have all of the facts."

"Then where does that leave Isabelle?" She asked, control-ling the anger that was beginning to simmer at Laroche and her father's seeming unwillingness to do anything.

"I'm sorry to have caused so much trouble," Isabelle said. "I can move to another country."

"That is not a solution," Dominique answered. "You will always be looking over your shoulder and will always be on the run. That is no way to live, especially with a child."

"Hashim may have parental rights with respect to Liam," Lidia suggested. "That could potentially put Isabelle in a position where she may be criminally responsible if she hides Liam from him, and she could lose him forever."

"Good point, Lidia," King Victor said. "As long as she is in Monteaux, we can protect her to some extent. But as I said, I do not want this to become an international event."

"We need to confirm whether these women are Ms. Balan and Ms. Eder and if Hashim has kidnapped them or if he is holding them against their will," Laroche said.

"If those girls were kidnapped from Klovia and Hashim is holding them against their will, President Balan could request a waiver of diplomatic immunity to prosecute Hashim," Victor added. "In that case, if President Balan is successful, Hashim will be in prison and will no longer be a threat to Isabelle."

"We should also verify whether he killed anyone and determine whether we can find evidence of that," Ethan suggested. "That would probably put Hashim in prison for much longer." He shifted his gaze to Isabelle. "Can you tell us anything about that, Isabelle?"

Dominique released a quiet breath, relieved at the turn the conversation was taking. She turned her focus to Isabelle.

She shook her head. "Hashim told me he had killed another girl who had given birth to his child because she disobeyed him. He said she tried to escape, and he had to make an example of her. He didn't say who she was."

"Wasn't there another college girl reported missing in addition to Dorina Eder?" Andre asked.

"Yes." Ethan nodded. "Maybe it was her that he killed."

"Where do we begin?" Dominique asked as she glanced

51

around the table, anxious to put a plan in place. "Any suggestions?"

"I think we have to start with the girls at Hashim's palace in Quam," Inspector Laroche replied.

"How do we do that?" Andre asked, turning to Ethan.

"We go there," Ethan answered. "We do recon. We try to find the girls and try to talk to them."

"And who is we?" King Victor asked. "I cannot allow anyone from my family to be a part of any recon in Quam," he began with a stern look at Dominique, "or any palace security," he added with a glance at Frederique, "or any Monteaux law enforcement," he finished with a look at Inspector Laroche. "I cannot risk Monteaux being involved at this point."

"I understand," Ethan replied with a nod.

"Father, I—"

"Stop." King Victor raised his hand, and his voice left no room for argument. "You are not going to Quam under any ruse you may concoct. I will, however," he lowered his hand and continued, "make available to Ethan any assistance he may need while in Monteaux, including providing whatever equipment he may require to take with him to Quam."

"Thank you, sir," Ethan replied. "That's very generous of you."

With a nod, Victor stood. "Lidia, shall we? I believe our presence is no longer needed here."

After Victor and Lidia left, Andre spoke. "Do you have a plan, Ethan?" he asked.

"I'm working on it," he replied. "And I think I'm going to have to call in a favor."

"If you need muscle," Inspector Laroche said, lifting a fist to his lips and clearing his throat, "let me know. I can give you a phone number."

"Can I find female muscle at that number?"

"I can see the wheels turning in your head," Andre remarked with a grin. "I want all the details on this recon mission, and I want to know what I can do from here."

"Sorry, bud," he replied. "That's top secret. And I'll let you know if I need you."

"What about the two men keeping surveillance outside?" Frederique asked. "They are likely Hashim's henchmen, and maybe Hashim is one of them. Would my handling of them have any bearing on your recon?"

"I think, for now, it's best if you leave them alone but keep them under surveillance. If you harass them, they may suspect you are doing so to protect Isabelle. If they think you are involved with her protection, Hashim might get nervous and do something with the girls in Quam. You should maintain the status quo with them while I'm in Quam, if you can."

"Will do," Frederique said with a nod. "We will make sure they don't attempt to get inside the walls here or harass any of our staff. I suppose as long as they are here, we know they are not in Quam or on their way there."

"I suspect they will get bored and leave on their own soon," Andre added.

Back in Dominique's suite, Ethan studied the maps and images Lance had sent to him. He was going to have to get to know Quam if he was going to be paying a visit to the country. The roads around Hashim's palace and every avenue of escape were going to need to be explored and memorized. He fought the distraction that threatened his concentration as Dominique paced the room and her lure pulled at him.

"Ethan, I don't like the idea of your going to Quam. That is not what I meant when I asked you to help me with Isabelle and Liam," she explained. "I only wanted you to use your software system to get information."

"The matter can't be resolved for Isabelle unless I go and confirm that the girls there are who we think they are and that they are there against their will."

"There must be another way. It is too dangerous for you to go to Quam."

"There isn't another way." He looked up when he saw her stop in front of him from the corner of his eye. "You heard your father. He doesn't want to contact President Balan until he is certain that his daughter is alive and being held against her will."

"My father doesn't have to tell him. You can go to President Balan and tell him."

"I can't tell President Balan anything without involving Monteaux. Isabelle and Liam are what led us to this point, and possibly his daughter, and they are here in your father's custody and care. Besides, even if I did tell President Balan, and he had his own men go to Quam, if it turns out that any of the girls there are not his daughter, or are missing, or are being held there against their will, it will put Isabelle in a far worse position. Hashim would know for certain that she and Liam are here. And, it would put your father in the middle of an international incident that he does not want. Besides, like your father said, he can protect Isabelle and Liam only to some extent."

"Then I think we should talk to my father about allowing me to go to Quam with you," she suggested. "I could help make contact with the girls. They may be more likely to trust you if I'm there. I can also cover you. From a safe distance. You know I've got a good aim."

"There are two things wrong with that idea," he answered as he looked back down and scribbled a few notes on a piece of paper. "First, I'd lose all credibility with your father and Andre, not to mention respect, if they thought I'd even consider risking your safety by taking you to Quam. Secondly,

I'm not going to risk your safety by taking you to Quam. Besides, I'm going to need Lance there, and he has no fighting skills. I'm going to have to keep him safe, not just have his back."

"There must be something I can do to help you in Quam without being in danger," she insisted.

"There isn't, and you're needed here," he replied, continuing with his notes. "You've kept Liam safe, you found Isabelle, and you're keeping them both safe now."

"They are safe simply by being inside the palace," she said, raising her voice as she stared down at him. "You wouldn't back me up at the meeting earlier and simply allowed my father to back out of doing anything because he didn't want to get his hands dirty. I need you to back me up about going to Quam. I need to do something other than sitting idly around."

He knew her well enough to know she didn't like having her hands tied when she perceived an injustice. He'd seen it in Washington, DC, when she had insisted on staying until they found out who had killed Jean Pierre. He knew she was near losing her patience, and he knew the best way to handle her temper was to ignore it, not be dismissive of her, and be reasonable.

"I understand where your father is coming from, and I agree with him." He stopped writing and looked up at her. "He really can't risk having a presence in Quam that is spying on the palace of the son of one of Quam's government officials. If anyone found out, it could put the entire principality of Monteaux at risk. There are political ramifications at play here."

"I am not a royal presence. I have been relieved of my royal duties."

He saw the anger smoldering behind her eyes, and he heard it in her voice.

"You are still a part of the royal family, and you are still a

Princess of Monteaux." He was sure he had just crossed over the line of reasonableness and stumbled into argumentative. "Isabelle is scared for herself and Liam, and she doesn't know what is going to happen next. I think she could use your support and help with Liam," he said, hoping to defuse the situation.

"Is that what you think?" she asked, glaring down at him. "That I should help take care of Liam, or are you just hoping that if I hang around him long enough, I'll change my mind about not wanting to have children?"

He wasn't sure how that topic got thrown in the mix, but he sure didn't like the inference in the question. He didn't enjoy being accused of trying to manipulate her into having children, and the thought that she would do that pricked at his patience. He tossed his pen aside and shot up to his feet.

"If you think that's my style, you don't know me as well as I thought you did. If I have to manipulate the person I love into doing something as important as having children, then it's not worth having children with her."

He saw the tears teetering in her eyes and suspected when she shot out of the room that she was upset about more than just having her hands tied with helping on the recon. When he heard the bedroom door slam shut, his suspicions were confirmed.

He dropped down to the chair. Damn, he thought, I'm going to have to end things soon. It isn't doing either of us any good delaying the inevitable. It's just gnawing away at us, driving us crazy.

CHAPTER EIGHT

Ethan spent the next couple of days studying videos, blue-prints and maps, tracking down a former female Israeli soldier for hire he had heard about from Laroche's contacts, and figuring out the logistics of securing the equipment he figured they'd need while he waited for Lance and Mike to arrive. He'd barely seen Dominique, and when he did, the tension between them was almost impenetrable, and the awkward-ness was, well, awkward. He didn't expect the recon to take more than four or five days, a week at most, and decided that when he returned, he and Dominique were going to have to finalize things between them. He wished there was another way, but they seemed trapped in this impasse between them, and ending things seemed like the only way out.

Lance was thrilled to be in the field, as he put it, and Mike was happy to help as long as he could be back home by Christ-mas. After they arrived, it took another day to put a plan in place and confirm everything with the former female Israeli soldier.

On the third day, it was a go. He grabbed the bag he'd packed and headed out of the bedroom. Dominique was wait-ing for him in the foyer of her suite. When she lifted her gaze to his, the heartache and fear on her face spoke volumes. He couldn't leave her like that, that much he knew. He could ease the fear, but the heartache was another story. He was dealing with it himself. He loved her. There was no doubt about that and no doubt that he wanted to spend the rest of his life with her. There was also no doubt that he had wanted children for as long as he could remember. Hell, he'd built a house to fill it with children. He was deeply afraid that if he gave up having children for her, he'd end up resenting her. If there was a chance of that, getting married would be setting up their relationship for failure. That was a risk not worth taking, in his book. It was better to end the relationship now than to waste years of their lives and have it end later.

He set his bag on the entry table and slid an arm around her waist. He pulled her into him and secured his other arm around her. He closed his eyes and breathed her in. He felt every inch of her as he held her against him. He felt her body yield and the tension between them melt like wax under a flame. No words were necessary. He felt it, and he knew she felt it.

"Be careful," she whispered and looked up at him.

"I'm always careful," he answered and touched his lips to hers, leaving a soft kiss. He released her, well aware it was the last thing he wanted to do, and grabbed his bag. He closed the door behind him and headed down the hall.

Dominique dropped to one of the chairs in her foyer, slid out of her shoes, and drew her legs to the seat. She rested her head against the wing of the chair and closed her eyes. She felt the heaviness of a dark cloud settle around her. She was frightened for Ethan, and Lance and Mike, as well. If they got caught, they would probably never come back. Justice in Arab countries was swift and lethal. She had never intended to put anyone at risk, and she prayed for their safe return.

The tension between her and Ethan had been replaced by a wedge. It was a steel door, and it was closing fast. Soon, she knew, it would be closed forever. She could not fathom a resolution between them, and she knew he couldn't. She'd heard it in his words, seen it in his eyes, and felt it in his heart. It would take a miracle to remove the wedge between them, and she prayed for that, too.

A knock at her door jolted her from her thoughts. It was either Lidia or Francine, she assumed. Only they ever came to her suite without calling ahead. She wasn't in the mood for a visitor, but if she was going to be interrupted, they were the ones she could tolerate at the moment.

She dragged herself up from the chair and forced herself to answer the door. She watched Lidia's smile dissolve when she opened the door.

"I came to check on you when I didn't see you downstairs. I've seen this look before," she said and entered the foyer, closing the door behind her. "And I know it's serious." She brushed aside a tress of Dominique's hair. "I'll make us some tea and meet you in the sitting room."

She nodded and headed to her sitting room. There was not a thing Lidia could do for her situation. She was sure of that, and she was pretty confident there was not a thing she could say to make her feel any better. She sunk into a chair, curled her legs under her, and waited for Lidia.

When she heard another knock at the door, she listened to voices but couldn't understand what they were saying. She assumed Lidia had requested something to be sent up from the kitchen, but Francine was crossing the threshold into the sitting room when she looked up.

"Hello, Dominique." Clearly, she was in a cheery mood, and she didn't want to ruin it, so she tried to force a smile in response. "I thought I'd see if you felt like doing a little shopping. I have just a few things to pick up before Christmas. Oh . . ." She frowned down at her. "You look miserable." She lowered herself to the edge of the chair facing her and put a hand on her knee. "Tell me, what happened? Are you worried about Ethan?"

"Francine, I brought an extra cup if you'd care to stay,"

Lidia announced as she entered the room carrying a tray.

"Only if I'm not interrupting," she replied, looking at Dominique for an answer and drawing her hand back.

"You're not interrupting," Dominique said. "But I must warn you both, I am not going to be good company, and if you stay, you are staying at your own risk. You could very well leave feeling deflated."

Lidia placed the tray on the table, circled around to the settee, and sat down.

Francine pushed back into the chair and tossed her jacket over the arm of the settee.

With all eyes on her, she began. "To answer your question, Francine, yes, I am worried about Ethan, but it's more than just that. I'm afraid Ethan and I disagree on a significant point, and it appears that we are unable to resolve the issue." She lowered her gaze and tried to hold her voice steady. "Our inability to come to terms on this issue leaves us with no choice but to end our relationship."

"What is the issue that has come between you?" Lidia asked, her voice calm and sympathetic.

She lifted her gaze and watched as Lidia poured the tea and then reached for a cup as she explained. "I just discovered that Ethan wants to have children. Lots of children. And Ethan just discovered that I do not want to have any children. Not one."

"You don't want children?" Francine asked, the surprise in her voice evident.

She shook her head and took a sip of tea. "No."

"Why don't you want children?" Lidia asked.

"The thought of it consumes me with terror." She searched Lidia's eyes for some sign that she understood, that she remembered.

"Emma?" Lidia asked, meeting her gaze.

She nodded.

"Who is Emma?" Francine asked.

"Emma was a baby doll that my mother had given me shortly before she passed away." She shifted her attention to Francine. "I took her everywhere with me. She had the sweetest face, and it was made of porcelain. My mother showed me how to take care of her, and she told me to be careful with her. And I was." She lowered her gaze as she felt the grief start to swell inside her. "Then my mother left us, and that baby doll became even more important to me. I felt like my mother had entrusted her to me when she left. I had to take care of her all by myself." She looked back up at Francine. "That baby doll kept a part of my mother alive for me. I knew as long as I was taking care of that baby doll as my mother had taught me, my mother was with me. We shared that doll when she was alive, and we shared her when she was gone."

She looked at Lidia and knew Lidia had remembered her pain as much as she did. She looked down and stared at the cup in her hands for a moment before she continued.

"Then, one day, I . . . I dropped her. She just fell out of my arms." She paused as she recalled the moment. "Her face shattered into a million pieces." She glanced up at Francine and then at Lidia. "And she was gone. And so was my mother." She shook her head and looked down. "There was nothing I could do to bring either of them back. I was devastated."

"She was inconsolable for months," Lidia added. "There was no replacing that baby doll or anything else she had lost."

"Is that why you never held my children?" Francine asked. "Or wouldn't sit with them for Andre and me?"

She looked up and nodded. "I was afraid and ashamed."

"So it isn't that you don't like children?"

"No. I like children. I just cannot get close to them. They fill me with fear. I know it's irrational, but the feelings are genuine."

"But, I've seen you with Liam. You're wonderful with him."

She smiled as she thought of Liam. "You've never seen me hold him, or feed him, or change him. The other day, before we found Isabelle, I was in the parlor alone with Liam, keeping an eye on him for the nanny. Before she came back, Ethan returned from Klovia and came into the parlor. He picked Liam up and played with him. Then he handed him to me and left to go upstairs. Liam started to squirm. I was petrified that I was going to drop him. All of the feelings of incompetence . . . and paralyzing fear . . . and shame . . . they all came flooding back."

"I see the significance of that doll to you and everything it represented, and, clearly, what happened to the doll was traumatic for you," Francine said.

Dominique studied her and saw that she was trying to understand what she had said and consider it all.

"But you cannot punish yourself for an unfortunate childhood accident."

"I'm not punishing myself."

"Can you remember how much you loved that baby doll, Dominique? Can you remember that feeling?" she asked.

"I suppose."

"That love multiplied a million times is the love that comes with children. Depriving yourself of that is punishment. And ending your relationship with Ethan is punishment."

"Not having that love and ending my relationship with Ethan is just a consequence. It's the consequence of not wanting children."

"No, my sweet, confused sister-in-law. It is not." The kindness and compassion in Francine's voice swept over her like a blanket of comfort. "That is the punishment you are giving yourself for the guilt and the shame you felt when you dropped your baby doll and destroyed something you loved and that kept you connected to your mother."

"I . . . don't . . . ." She couldn't find the words and looked at

Lidia. She was there. She would understand.

"You must forgive yourself, Dominique," Lidia said. "Your mother did not go away when you dropped your doll. She has always been with you. Have children and share them with your mother."

"It is not meant to be. I have no maternal instincts."

"You've been telling yourself that for a long time," Francine said. "It's not surprising that you believe it. No mother has maternal instincts, Dominique. We don't magically know everything just because we can get pregnant. You just have to pay attention to your baby, and you'll learn what it needs. And if you can't figure it out, you hire a nanny. You don't know this, but when I had your nephew, I was so afraid I was starving him to death because I couldn't measure how much milk he was getting when I was nursing him. I finally gave up and fed him formula, so I could see how much was in the bottle. And when he was four months old, I took him to the doctor because he was hungry all the time. Do you know what the doctor told me? She told me to feed him. I didn't know I was to have started him on cereal. That's when I hired a nanny." When Francine reached over and took her hand, a sense of relief settled around her. "And children are not made of porcelain. Most of the time, they do not break when you drop them or when they fall. They are terribly resilient." She released a sigh and drew her hand back. "My dear Dominique, you have placed way too much pressure on yourself. It is no wonder you are terrified."

"I don't know," she said. It all felt overwhelming yet reassuring at the same time. "I don't know about any of this. I don't know if I can change twenty-four years of feeling this way."

"Why don't we test that," Lidia suggested. "Isabelle and Liam aren't going anywhere right now. Why don't you spend some time with them? I'm sure Isabelle can use the help now that the nanny is back full time with Francine's children."

"Do you think I can change how I feel about having children, Lidia?" If it was a possibility, she would try. Especially if it meant saving her relationship with Ethan.

"I do with all my heart, Dominique. It's not really a question of whether you *want* children. It's a question of whether you can overcome your fear that you will break them."

"You are a strong woman, Dominique," Francine reminded her. "I've watched you overcome worse things."

CHAPTER NINE

It was the start of day three of the recon, and Ethan felt his patience being tested. It was hot in the van, the days were long, and they weren't making much progress. To make matters worse, he was getting distracted by thoughts of Dominique. He reminded himself that he would put himself and everyone with him in danger if he lost his concentration. He couldn't do anything about Dominique while he was in Quam anyway, he told himself and shoved her out of his mind.

He looked over at Liel. With four of them in the van, and one being a woman, the quarters were especially tight. She was turning out to be a good asset, though. She'd managed to get into Quam with a decent collection of weapons. He'd been lucky to find her, he figured, surprised by the quality of contacts Laroche had for this level of work.

"Maybe we should start coming up with a plan to get inside the palace to make contact instead of waiting for one of them to come out," Mike suggested.

Ethan shook his head. "I don't know. I think it's too risky. Even if the girls are being held against their will, if we scare them, they could blow our cover unintentionally."

"Hold on," Lance said, peering down at the laptop monitor. "It looks like one of the girls is putting on a niqab. She must be going out."

"It's about time," Mike muttered.

"Liel," Ethan began.

"Getting dressed," she answered.

"Which girl, Lance?" he asked.

"The one that looks like Bianca."

"I'll watch the monitor," he said, nudging Lance. "Get the earbuds and mics, and recheck them."

"Okay, boss." When Lance moved aside, he glanced over to make sure he dug into the right duffle bag. Satisfied, he turned his gaze to the monitor.

He watched the girl as she moved in and out of view of the palace security cameras. When she exited the front entrance, he alerted Mike. "She's getting into one of the black *Mercedeses.* There's a driver and someone riding shotgun. She's in the back."

"I wouldn't think two guards would be needed unless she is being protected or held captive," Mike remarked. "And, here we go," he added as he turned over the engine. They waited for a visual of the *Mercedes,* and when the gates to the palace opened and the car pulled into the street, Mike steered into the same lane a few cars behind the *Mercedes.*

He closed the laptop and dragged a duffle bag to his feet. He pulled out a *Glock 19,* checked it, loaded it, and then handed it to Liel.

"Thanks," she said and tucked it under her abaya. "I usually carry a knife, as well," she said and extended a hand.

He reached back into the bag, tugged out a sheath containing a knife, and handed it to her. He watched as she strapped it to her leg.

"I'll have your back," he reminded her.

She smiled over at him as she adjusted her abaya. "And I'll have yours."

He grinned and nodded back, then checked and loaded another *Glock 19.* He snapped a holster to his belt and slid the pistol in it. Then he reached into his pocket, slid out a folding knife, and flicked his wrist. The blade snapped open. He squeezed it closed and shoved it back in his pocket.

"Boss . . . um . . . I know Mike's hanging back with me . . . but, you know, last time . . . um . . . is there anything in there for me?"

A smile cut across his face as he grabbed a *Smith and Wesson* revolver from the duffle bag. "Merry Christmas," he said, handing it to Lance. "It's loaded, and there's no safety. All you have to do is point and shoot. It's ready to go, so be careful."

"Thanks, boss." He turned it over in his hands, admiring it. "How many shots do I get?"

"You better hit something on your sixth try."

"Looks like she's going shopping," Mike said, and Ethan looked up as he turned the van into a parking lot.

"Lance, pin the camera on Liel's niqab."

"Yeah, boss."

"Are you ready, Liel?" he asked.

"Roger that," she replied with a wink.

"Looks like a market," Mike said, pulling into a space. "The car's on the curb, letting her out," he said with a nod toward the front of the market.

Ethan slid the van door open, and Liel stepped out. Without hesitation, she headed to the entrance to the market. Ethan watched her as she walked through the parking lot, passed behind the *Mercedes,* and entered the store.

"Looks like they're both staying in the car," Mike said. "They're probably not supposed to let her out of their sight. Lucky for us, they're lazy assholes."

"Yeah, but I'm still going in," he said and stepped from the van. "Let me know if anything changes," he said and slid the door closed.

Making his way through the parking lot, he heard Liel's voice in his earpiece. "Are you Bianca Balan from Klovia?" Her voice was quiet and calm.

"Who are you?" was the panicked response he heard. "I could get in trouble if anyone recognizes me. Please, don't say my name."

He continued listening to the conversation as he entered the market.

"Are you being held against your will?" Liel pressed on.

He assumed the response must have been a nod when Liel continued.

"How many other girls are being held captive with you?"

"Please, don't talk to me. It's too dangerous. There could be spies here."

"Take this," he heard Liel say. "If anyone asks what we were talking about, tell them I gave you this pamphlet and was talking to you about Christianity. How many girls are being held captive with you?"

"One other, and we each have a child." Her voice was barely above a whisper. He hoped Lance was able to pick it up on the recorder. "And there is a third child. Who are you?"

"We are putting a rescue in place. How many guards are in residence at the palace?"

"No." The panic in her voice peaked. "If you fail, we will be killed."

"You are safe." He heard Liel assure her, and then he stepped into their line of vision. He observed them in the produce department as they appeared to select fruit, but he gave no indication that he was watching them. "That man is keeping us safe in here," she said with a nod toward him. "There are two other men outside watching the two guards who brought you here. I can hear everything the men say, and they will warn me if your guards leave the car. Was someone killed for attempting to escape?"

He saw Bianca nod and then heard her whisper. "In front of us, to show us what will happen if we try to escape."

"What is the name of the other girl who is being held with you?"

"Dorina Eder."

"How many guards reside at the palace?"

"Five right now, but when Hashim comes to visit, he brings more."

"How many staff reside at the palace?"

"Four, but that number increases, too, when Hashim comes."

"Do you know when he is to come next?"

"No. He never tells us."

"If I give you a small listening device, can you place it in the guard's office?"

"No," she replied, the panic in her voice rising again. "I can't risk it."

"One of the guards has exited the car." Mike's voice spilled into his earpiece, and when he glanced at Liel, he saw her slide a hand down over the pistol concealed under her abaya. "Looks like he's just stretching his legs, but you better hurry it up."

"How can I get in touch with you?" Liel asked. "Are you allowed to leave the palace?"

"We are only allowed to come here to buy the food we want to eat. I am brought on Mondays, and Dorina is brought on Thursdays, but the time varies."

"Can you reveal your face so I can get you on camera?"

Ethan watched as she pulled at her niqab and then readjusted it.

"Let Dorina know about us so she won't be surprised if we contact her here."

"When will you be back?"

"Soon."

Dominique smiled at Isabelle and Liam as Isabelle bounced Liam on her lap, making him erupt in a fit of giggles. Francine and Lidia had given her much to consider, and if their advice could help her overcome her fear of having children, she would follow it.

"I am still not comfortable with staying here as a guest," Isabelle said. "I feel like I have taken advantage of you, and the staff feels that way, too. I heard them talking. They think I should still be working even if I am hiding out here. And I agree. After all, I am an employee here. If I worked, I could pay Francine's nanny to sit with Liam while I work." She settled Liam on her lap and continued. "I did not mean for things to get so out of hand. I was just waiting for Hashim's men to leave so I could escape with Liam. And look what I've done."

Dominique watched as tears filled Isabelle's eyes.

"I've put the entire palace in danger with those men camped out there, and Mr. Moore, I am so worried about him. What am I doing here?" she asked as tears spilled onto her cheeks and Liam started crying. "Oh, no, Liam. It's okay."

She pushed herself up and then sat down beside Isabelle and Liam. She put an arm around Isabelle's shoulder. "Shh. It's going to be all right. We have security here protecting us, and Mr. Moore is trained to do exactly what he is doing."

Liam released a healthy wail, and she felt Isabelle shudder before she broke down in sobs.

She drew her arm from Isabelle's shoulder and took Liam from her. She situated him securely in her lap, wrapped an arm around him, and lifted a hand to Isabelle's chin. "You listen to me, Isabelle. You and Liam are exactly where you are meant to be. I want you to go to your room, fill your tub, step in it, close your eyes, and relax. When you are feeling better, I want you to take a nap. When you wake up, I want you to order yourself some dinner and have it sent to your room."

"But . . .Liam," she managed between her quivers and his wails.

"I will take care of Liam, and he will be fine," she said it as much to convince Isabelle as to convince herself. "We'll talk later when Liam is down for the night."

Isabelle nodded, dragged a sleeve across her eyes, and then got up. When she was gone, she turned Liam to her and looked him in the eyes.

"Look at me, baby," she said. Her voice was a soft, soothing river of calm. "Look at me, baby," she repeated. "Liam," she whispered his name, and his wails subsided to whimpers as he stared back at her. "That's it, Liam." She plucked the scarf from around her neck and dabbed at his tears. "I've got you," she continued as she waited for the whimpers to wane. "You're going to be fine, Liam," she cooed as she watched his bottom lip turn down and tremble. "We're almost there." When he glanced at the scarf and reached for it, she spoke again. "You can have it, Liam." He looked back up at her and then tugged at the scarf. "Are we ready to play?" she asked, and when she dragged the scarf over his head, she heard a giggle. When it dropped in his lap, she saw a smile. *Not only is he still alive, but I've calmed him. Maybe I can take care of him.* She hoped.

She managed to entertain Liam with the scarf for longer than she expected as she thought of new things to do with it. When he finally got bored with the scarf, she read him some children's books from her niece and nephew's library. A few hours had passed when he finally fell asleep in her arms. She carried him to the bassinette and laid him inside. He had survived her, or she had survived him, or both. He hadn't been that challenging, and she had managed to be alone with him without panicking.

She looked up when she heard someone enter the parlor. Francine strolled toward her, a smile gracing her face. "I heard you were in here alone with the baby." She stopped when she reached the bassinette and peered inside. "He looks like he's in one piece to me, and not a bruise on him."

"As it turns out, playing with a baby isn't that difficult if you can keep him occupied," she replied.

"From what I was told, you did a little more than just play with him," Francine said as she sat down. "Give yourself some credit. You're making strides here. By the way, will you be joining the family tonight for the annual Christmas tree lighting ceremony at the lake?"

"I forgot about that. I'm going to have to miss it. I need to help Isabelle with something."

"Oh?" Francine lifted a brow. "Would that something be Liam?"

"Indirectly, I suppose."

"Darn," Francine said with a frown when her phone chimed. "I need to tend to something. I'll see you at dinner," she said, pushing herself up, "and remember, dinner will be served earlier tonight because of the ceremony."

CHAPTER TEN

"President Balan, sir," Ethan began as he extended his hand to him, "thank you for meeting with us on such short notice."

"When His Majesty, the King of Monteaux, requests a meeting with someone and says it is urgent, I'm not going to question it," he replied, accepting his hand. "Please take a seat. If this is urgent, let's get on with it. What is this about?"

"Please allow me to introduce my team. This is Mike Gardner, a former US Army Special Forces member," he said with a nod toward Mike. "Liel David, a former member of the Israel Defense combat intelligence," he said as he gestured toward her. "And Lance Meyers, Chief Assistant at ESM Defense," he finished with a nod toward Lance.

"It's nice to meet you all," President Balan replied.

"Sir," Ethan began as he lowered himself to a chair. "We've just come back from a recon mission in Quam."

"What does that have to do with me?"

"This, sir," he said and placed a small recorder on the table. Liel's and Bianca's voices filled the room when he pressed a button.

"What kind of a joke is this?" the President demanded, leaping to his feet.

"It is no joke, sir," Liel said, rising to hers. "That is my voice on the recording, and it was made this morning with your daughter, Bianca."

Ethan placed the photograph of Bianca on the table before him.

"I took that photograph of her this morning, too," Liel reported.

"She's really alive?" he asked in disbelief, lifting the photograph from the table.

"Yes, sir," Ethan replied. "As Bianca said on the tape, she, another girl, and three small children are being held captive in Quam. The Hashim individual mentioned on the tape is Hashim Aziz, the son of the Quam ambassador here in Klovia, Masoud Aziz. They are being held in Hashim Aziz's palace."

"That son of a bitch," he seethed.

"As I mentioned, sir, our mission was strictly recon, not rescue. We are here to provide you with information. We assume you will employ Klovia's military to conduct a rescue mission."

"And, sir," Liel added, "I would be willing to participate in that mission, if you like, given that I have made contact with your daughter and she appears to trust me."

"Of course, of course, yes," the President replied.

"Sir, we would be happy to meet with your general if you would like us to brief him," he suggested. "We also have blueprints of the palace and maps of the surrounding area that we would be happy to provide."

He nodded and turned to his aide. "Tell General Pichler to come to my office immediately," he ordered. "And Counselor Stoian, as well." He glanced around the table. "I can't thank you enough for finding my daughter. What can I do for you in return?"

"All I ask, sir, is that you request that diplomatic immunity be waived for Hashim Aziz and that he be dealt with harshly. Your daughter and the other young women he has threatened will need protection from him. And I would suggest that monetary retribution be provided to his victims."

A slight laugh escaped the President's lips. "He'll be dealt with harshly," he said with a nod. "You have my word. And whatever his victims need, they will be provided."

LaBuerge Palace was quiet with the family and most of the staff attending the annual Christmas tree lighting ceremony. Dominique observed that Isabelle was much more relaxed after some time to herself. The assault on Mrs. Bardot and the stress of Hashim's men camped outside of the palace had frazzled her nerves and taken a toll on her, but it was almost over. The palace security had reported earlier that the two men watching the palace had left, and Ethan had reported to her father that Hashim's fate was now in the hands of President Balan.

Liam had finally fallen asleep in her arms for a second time that day, so Dominique placed him in the bassinette and joined Isabelle in front of the fire. She couldn't wait to update Isabelle and let her know that she would soon be free of Hashim.

"I have good news for you," she began.

"You do?"

"Yes, I — " She was interrupted when Isabelle's gaze turned abruptly toward the doorway and she rushed over to the bassinette. As she turned to see what had drawn Isabelle's attention, she witnessed a dark figure approaching Isabelle. When he reached the bassinette, he grabbed her arm.

"Stay away from us," Isabelle demanded before biting down on the man's arm. In response, the man released his grip and slammed his arm against her head, sending her sailing into a table before collapsing onto the floor.

When she saw the man peer into the bassinette, the need to protect Liam had her grabbing a fireplace poker. She bolted toward the man, and before he could place a hand on Liam, she swung the fire iron with the force of a major league hitter. The end of the fire iron struck its target dead center. The man fell backward onto the floor, the poker firmly planted in his skull.

She took a step toward Isabelle. *"Two, there were two,"* echoed in her head, and she retreated to the fireplace. She snatched a second fire iron from the tool stand and rushed to the doorway. Pressed against the giant wooden soldier, she raised the poker poised to attack and waited. Her chest heaved with each frantic breath as her heart pounded inside it.

Her gaze caught a foot stepping across the threshold. She wielded the iron, but its mark was quicker than the last one. The poker was torn from her grip and tossed aside. A hand circled her neck and brought her to her knees, then pushed her onto the floor. The dark stare of a man burned into her gaze. She saw the venom smoldering in his eyes. She reached for his face and dug her nails in deep. She delivered a foot to his chest when he pulled back, releasing his grasp from her neck. She sucked in a breath and struggled to push up. He administered a back-handed strike to the side of her head and sent her back down. Dazed from the hit, she fought to focus as her eyes fluttered closed.

Isabelle's moan from across the room and thoughts of Liam had her forcing her eyes open. When she stared up through the fog, she saw movement beside her as the assailant took a step away. He was headed in Liam's direction. She pushed herself over and closed her hands around the assailant's ankle, tripping him up and bringing him down. He hit the floor with a thud and a groan. She felt a knife attached to his ankle under her fingers and snatched it loose.

While he was still down, she lunged on top of him, hoping to gain the advantage, but miscalculating his prowess. In one quick move, she was beneath him, and his hands were around her neck once again. She curled her fingers around the knife, ready to slice, when he smiled down at her and her vision started to blur. Above him, she saw a figure snap his neck and thrust his lifeless body aside.

"Dominique, are you all right?" Ethan's panicked voice swept over her, and his face came into focus above her.

She nodded and pointed toward the table. "Isabelle," she managed between breaths and heard the clamor of footsteps enter the parlor.

She saw Ethan look in the direction of the table, then back at her. "They've got her."

"Liam," she said and struggled to get up.

She felt Ethan's arms under her as he lifted her from the floor and helped her get to the bassinette. Liam's eyes were closed when she looked inside, and he was still. As she stared down at him, she saw his lips tremble, then lift to a smile.

"He's dreaming," Ethan said.

"My . . . Lord." She turned when she heard her father's voice explode through the room. "What is going on in here?" He was standing in the doorway surveying the aftermath. "Take the women out of here," he ordered, and she watched as Francine and Lidia were ushered out of sight.

"It looks like Hashim's men may not have gotten word that his reign is over, Your Majesty," Ethan answered, glancing over at the body with the poker.

"Dominique, are you all right?" her father asked, making his way toward her as she tried to get to Isabelle.

"I'm fine, Father," she assured him.

"And Isabelle? Is she all right?" he asked. "And the baby?"

"Dominique?" she heard Isabelle's voice over the guards huddled around her.

"Liam's fine," she called back to her as she broke through the huddle.

"She may have a concussion, and she needs stitches," one of the guards said. "We're taking her to the hospital."

"Dominique?" Isabelle said, reaching for her.

"Liam's fine," she assured her again, taking her hand. "I'll take care of him. Let them take you to the hospital. You'll be all right. It's over." She glanced over at Ethan, and he nodded. "It's all over. You and Liam are safe now."

"Frederique." She heard her father call to him. "Call Inspector Laroche and get him over here."

"How did President Balan say he was going to handle the matter with Hashim?" Dominique asked once things had settled down and they were headed up to her wing. Despite the horror of the evening's events, there was a silver lining there that lifted her spirits and she couldn't wait to share it with Ethan.

"He wasn't specific, but I can tell you that Hashim's days on this earth are numbered if they are not over as we speak," Ethan replied.

"That's such a relief. So Isabelle is free to return to Klovia if she wants to?"

"She is free to do whatever she wants, and she and Liam will be financially provided for."

"By whom?"

"Most likely the government of Quam."

"That will be a bit of unexpected good news to tell her when she gets back from the hospital tomorrow." She turned to the two attendants who followed them to her suite as she opened the door. "Please follow me. I'll show you which room to put him in." She continued to one of the guest rooms, then gestured to the attendants. "You may put him in here."

"Yes, Your Royal Highness," they replied as they lowered the bassinette.

"Thank you," she responded and leaned in to peek at Liam as they left.

"I must say this is surprising for someone that doesn't want to have children," Ethan remarked as he stared into the bassinette over her shoulder.

"Oh, that's all changed," she replied as she retreated from the room. "Can I make you a drink?" she asked, glancing at him over her shoulder. "After all, it is the holidays."

"How about I make you one?" he suggested, following her into a small parlor. "From what I saw, it looked like you had quite an exhausting evening."

"That would be nice. It was a little tiring." She lowered herself to the sofa and watched him continue to the bar. After mixing their drinks, he joined her on the sofa and handed her a glass.

"That's all changed?" he asked, raising a brow. "Care to elaborate?"

"I would, thank you," she replied. She took a sip of her drink, then began. "The reason that I did not want children is that I am terrified that I cannot take care of them, and that if they are left in my care, they will end up very badly injured if they survive at all. In your absence, Francine and Lidia assessed the underlying psychological basis for my fears, and they explained to me that my fears are unfounded. In addition, in your absence, I made efforts to physically care for Liam and discovered that I could play with a baby without causing him harm. More importantly, tonight I saved Liam from harm, which has given me quite a bit of confidence. So, to answer your question, what has changed is that I do want children, and I will have children with you." She saw a mix of relief and joy in his eyes as she continued. "But I must warn you that I'm am going to need help taking care of them. I am more comfortable now and more confident, but there is still much I need to learn."

"I had no idea that the reason you didn't want children was based on fear, and I'm grateful that you're trying to overcome that fear." He placed a hand on her arm and his voice firmed. "I promise you, you don't need to be afraid. I will help you take care of our children, and I will teach you what I know. And what I don't know and what you don't know, we will learn together."

"I think if we're going to be parents, we should start getting our rest," she suggested. "Shall we go to the bedroom?"

"I'd have to agree, and yes."

"I'll check on Liam and meet you in there."

When she got to the bedroom, she noticed Ethan had already exchanged his clothes for a robe and was lighting a fire. She headed to her dressing room, then disappeared while she slipped into a short, silk robe. She adjusted the tie as she walked over to the bed and then sat on the edge. She watched him as he stoked the fire. She scooted onto the bed and then leaned back against the headboard.

"It's getting warm in here," he remarked as he turned from the fireplace and tugged the belt loose on his robe. "Can I get you anything?"

"Just you." She studied him as he sauntered across the room. With each step, she caught a glimpse of the naked flesh and cut muscle of a well-endowed man. And with each step, she felt his pull. It was impossible to resist.

"I'm all yours." When he lifted his robe off his shoulders and let it slide down his arms and onto the floor, she felt her heart skip a beat.

"Nice to know."

He lay down on the bed, then rolled over to face her. He propped up on an elbow, reached over, and tugged the tie on her robe loose. When it fell open, all the lovely tiny nerves just below the surface of her skin stirred. And when his fingers skimmed over her bare flesh as they traveled between her breasts, little urges pulsed through her.

He pulled her down to him and took her mouth in his. She could taste the desire whipping through him. When he drew her closer, and their bodies melded, urges and desires turned to need.

He dragged his tongue down her neck and over her breasts. She reached for him and cupped her hand between his legs. He retook her mouth, and she rolled on top of him. She spread her legs, and he pushed inside her.

She pulled up nearly off of him and then slid back down the length of him. She pulled away, then filled herself with him again, savoring each movement.

His arm circled her, and in an instant, he flipped her beneath him. "Don't move," he whispered, still inside her. He reached for her legs, lifted them to his sides, and leaned over her. "Stay still," he whispered as he slowly pulled back, then slid back in. With each drive, she thought she would go mad as she resisted the urge to move as need turned to desperation.

At his mercy, he pushed her to the edge. A million roaring waves of lust crashed inside her with his final entry.

CHAPTER ELEVEN

"I heard from Isabelle yesterday," Dominique announced to the family as they gathered in the parlor to open Christmas gifts. "She is getting along nicely with Bianca and Dorina, and she said Liam seems to be enjoying his half-siblings. In fact, they are all celebrating Christmas together."

"I'm happy that everything turned out well for her," Francine said.

"Despite everything, I think she turned out to be a blessing in disguise," Lidia added.

"I don't know about that," Victor remarked. "But today certainly is a blessing, so let's celebrate." He handed Lidia a large package wrapped in silver and gold paper adorned with a red bow. "Let's open some gifts." He glanced over at Ethan and tossed him a wink.

"Good idea, Father," Andre replied as he handed Francine a gift.

"This is for you," Ethan said and gave Dominique a small box wrapped with a silver bow.

"What is it?" she asked, tugging the bow loose. She opened the box and stared at the sparkling diamond and platinum ring, unsure what it meant.

"Will you marry me?" he whispered.

Her heart gave an unexpected little start when she grasped what was happening. She managed a nod as tears spilled onto her cheeks, and he placed the ring on her finger.

"I'd like to make a toast to the engaged couple," Victor announced, raising a glass of champagne.

ABOUT THE AUTHOR

Josephine Valent has lived and worked for most of her life in Southern California at the beach, in the city, in the country, and most recently, in the desert, which she now calls home. She enjoys taking cross-country road trips and has traveled coast to coast several times.

An avid reader growing up, she considers it liberating to open a book, leave life behind, and step into someone else's world.

When she's not immersed in the lives of the heroines she's conjuring up for her next romance novels, she's watching true crime shows.

She loves romance, dares to dream, and writes as if anything is possible and she is limited only by her imagination.

www.ingramcontent.com/pod-product-compliance
Lightning Source LLC
Chambersburg PA
CBHW071342130626
46556CB00005B/1984